THE TRIALS OF ILDARWOOD

ORIGINS

CINDERS IN THE SNOW

S. C. SELVYN

AVYLAAN KINGDOM PRESS LLC

Provincetown, MA

ISBN: 978-1-963205-00-8 (Paperback, Amazon KDP)
ISBN: 978-1-64365-097-5 (Paperback, IngramSpark)
ISBN: 978-1-64365-098-2 (Hardcover)

Library of Congress Control Number: 2023921890

This book is a work of fiction. All names, characters, places, and events are products of the author's imagination, and any resemblances to actual events or places or persons, living or dead, is entirely coincidental.

Cover illustration by Jeff Brown.
Map illustration by Chaim Holtjer.
Chapter illustrations by David Perez.
Copyediting by Leonora Stewart.
Proofreading by Katie Bucklein.
Book design by Lisa Vega.
Typesetting by Emily Snyder.
Sensitivity reading by Anna Everts, Gabriel Hargrave, and Rue Dickey.

Printed in the United States of America.

First edition published December 2023.

Avylaan Kingdom Press LLC
PO BOX 190
Raynham Center, MA 02768

www.theildarwood.com

For every person forced to live their life behind a veil
and every soul who never had the chance to right their tale.

In loving memory of

Joshua,

a childhood friend,
whose story ended far too soon.

TABLE OF CONTENTS

❧ LORE OF THE ILDARWOOD ❧

A Note from the Author

For over twenty years, this particular origin story has been very special to me. Right before I published the first book in this series, however, I learned of the unexpected passing of a childhood friend—the one who had inspired me to create the character of Tannus Ambers.

At around the same time, I learned of another tragic passing in my hometown—this time, a teenager I did not know personally. All they ever wanted was to be their most authentic self, but regrettably, the world around them had been far too cruel.

Though entirely unrelated to each other, both cases reminded me why it was so important to tell the stories of a variety of characters throughout this series. Like most of us, they aren't on some fantastical adventure to save the world. They only care about saving the world that matters most to them—the one they interact with every day, involving their families, their friends, their communities, or even just themselves. Theirs are struggles we can all relate to in some way, perhaps far more than we can to so many other fictional stories we might read.

That's why I truly hope these books will one day save a reader's life. Whether they realize it or not, every single person has within themselves a gift that the world may never see again, as well as a light that, once extinguished, will leave the life of everyone who ever loved them far less bright.

The story ahead may not be for everyone, and it may hit a little too close to home for others. But if you are the one reader whose life takes a turn back toward hope after reading it, then no matter what passing storms a tale like this one may stir for me personally, publishing this book will have been worth it.

S. C. Selvyn

CONTENT WARNING

Certain scenes in this novel include depictions of emotional abuse and various forms of discrimination against marginalized communities, which some readers may find distressing.

These scenes are limited in the main story but are more prevalent in the final chapters of lore, where the historical struggles of these communities are used to illustrate the subsequent progress made to largely overcome and eliminate such mistreatment in this fictional world.

Sensitivity readers were hired to review all such content. However, reader discretion is still advised.

For more details, please visit:

www.theildarwood.com/notices

FOR ADVENTUROUS READERS

This novel includes three chapters of ancient lore after the epilogue.

They provide self-contained short stories
about the history of this world.

For exclusive content, full-color illustrations, and a
high-definition version of the map of Ranewood, please visit:

www.theildarwood.com

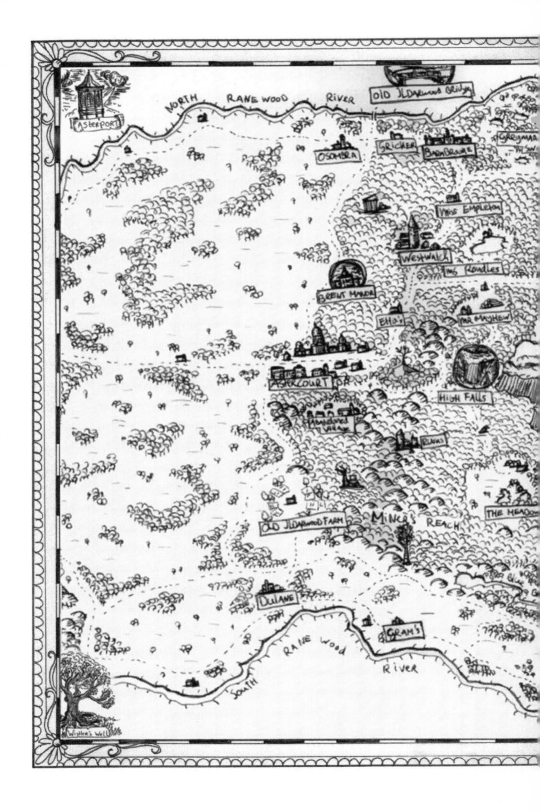

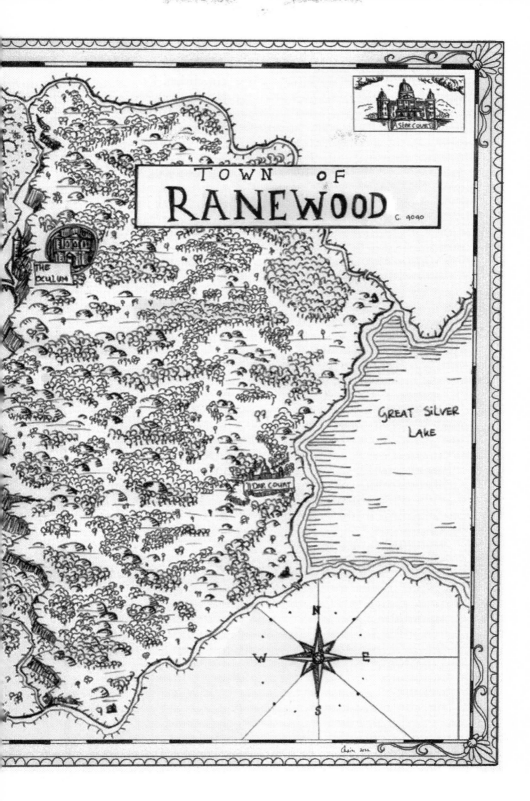

Prologue

S NOW NEVER STOPPED falling inside the house of little Dasia
Dulane—not once since her brother Dustane was first born. Or so
her parents always said.

Like fine prismatic crystals, the shimmering flecks tumbled gently
down from a swirling sphere of pale blue flames, which floated ever so
effortlessly in the silver-domed structure on the roof. Casting a haunting light upon the sparkling Ildarwood tree that grew directly up from
the center of the house, the radiant spectral star had long protected the
Dulanes from every manner of threat to their modest swampside dwell-
ing. But not until Dustane was first brought home did the ever-watchful
Ildarstar begin to weep its frost-born tears, creating a breathtaking display of his family's newfound sorrow.

Nine long years had Dasia spent with her family in the unnatural
cold of their cheerless cottage, which stood on the southernmost border
of the impoverished town of Marshwood. A squalid settlement if ever
there was one, it was forever forced to wade within the vast, fetid swamp
just north of the once-great city of Silvermarsh.

Long had Dasia dreamed of escaping that wretched place and

finding somewhere far less depressing to live. In fact, it was the only dream she shared with every other member of her silver-haired family, including her beloved older brother, Demitris. So every now and again, Dasia would join her parents and Demitris on their rickety front porch, where they would each stare longingly at all the twinkling silver lights above the ancient city on the horizon—each and every radiant flicker, some happy family's vibrant Ildarstar.

"One day," her mother and father would often say, "we will *finally* save enough money to move away from this awful town and all the miserable people in it."

"What about Dustane?" Dasia once asked nervously. "Can he come too?"

Silence followed as Mr. and Mrs. Dulane exchanged furtive glances. Then their gazes drifted upward ever so reluctantly in the direction of a perpetually locked attic door.

"We don't have a choice," Mrs. Dulane answered. "We can't exactly leave him here."

Yet from the dour expressions upon her parents' faces, Dasia could tell there was not a single thing in life the two regretted more—that is, until the fall of 9087, when the entire family was forced to watch helplessly as Silvermarsh City was overrun by violent riots and golden flames.

The spectral snow in Dasia's house fell especially hard for months thereafter, even during the hottest days of summer that next year. But a renewed sense of hope arrived in the fall of 9088, when Mr. and Mrs. Dulane proudly announced that they had finally saved enough Silver Starlings to escape the foul swamp of Marshwood. But instead of taking their children to Silvermarsh, or even the quiet town of Ranewood, just beyond, Mr. and Mrs. Dulane brought them to the esteemed settlement of Amberdale, further south.

Beaming with joy as they entered their stately new home atop a wooded lakeside hill, Mr. and Mrs. Dulane could hardly believe that their dreams had finally come true.

"We're all really gonna live here?" Dasia asked with awe as she stared into the cavernous entrance hall, very nearly convinced that their old Marshwood home could have fit snugly inside.

"I can't believe there's no snow," said Demitris, his sparkling silver eyes wide with amazement.

"And hopefully, there won't be any from now on," Mr. Dulane promptly replied.

"Can we go see our rooms?" Dasia asked gleefully.

"Of course you can," said Mrs. Dulane. "They're just upstairs, to the left."

After racing each other up the home's twin spiral staircases—Dasia to the left and Demitris to the right—the two did not stop until each stood proudly within their very own room.

"Wow! I can actually see the lake from here!" Dasia shouted from beside her towering windows.

"Just a little bit nicer than your old view of the swamp, now, isn't it?" Mrs. Dulane replied.

"So much better," Dasia answered with a smile. But her elation turned abruptly to sorrow when she noticed the unusual door on one side of the room. Protected by a thick, sparkling layer of Ildarglass, it had been expertly embellished with an elaborate eight-point star design— just like the hidden door to the attic in their old Marshwood home.

"That's where Dustane's supposed to live, isn't it?" Dasia asked her mother, who nodded solemnly in response before approaching her daughter from behind.

"You're the only one who can stop him from getting out, so we need you to make sure he never does." Placing her frigid hands on Dasia's shoulders, Mrs. Dulane was intent on making sure her daughter fully understood the importance of her warning. "If anyone ever finds out about him, it'll be the end of our family, and everything we've spent our entire lives working toward will all be taken away. Understand?"

Dasia's heart broke as the burden placed upon her finally began to sink in. "Can't I at least let him out when no one's around?" she asked timidly.

"We just can't take that risk. It's too dangerous, and so is he. That's why I really need you to promise you will *never* let him out." And with those words, Mrs. Dulane squeezed her daughter's shoulders, sending an unnatural chill down Dasia's spine.

"I promise," said Dasia, her lips and eyes turning a haunting shade of blue.

"Good. Now go ahead and seal the door, just like we taught you."

Dasia took a single step forward with great reluctance, then reached out toward the ornate silver doorknob. "Please don't make me do this," she said softly, her delicate fingers lingering just a few inches away from its polished surface.

"It has to be you," Mrs. Dulane insisted. "Your two souls are connected in a way that makes it impossible for us to lock him away without your help. So you need to decide, right here and now: will you help us keep this family safe, or will we need to lock *you* away too?"

A single sparkling tear fell from Dasia's cheek as she stood between her mother and the door. Watching as the tiny droplet evaporated into a fine spectral mist, she wondered if Dustane would ever truly be allowed to run free.

"Please don't do it," a weak voice called out from somewhere within, breaking Dasia's heart even more.

"I'm so sorry," Dasia whispered. Only then did she grab ahold of the ornate silver knob, causing the entire door to light up with a momentary pale blue glow as a haunting frost appeared upon its surface. An instant later, a thunderous click echoed out, making it painfully clear that the door had at last been locked.

"I know that wasn't easy," said Mrs. Dulane, who finally eased her viselike grip. "But I'm very, very proud of you."

Dasia turned to face her mother but could not bear to look her in the eye. All she could manage was a weak, dispirited sigh. A subtle gasp from Mrs. Dulane immediately followed, for despite the mild autumn air flowing gently throughout the room, a ghostly haze lingered briefly before young Dasia, sparkling and still.

"Not again," Mrs. Dulane whispered as she swiftly searched the ceiling for any subtle signs of spectral snow. "I'll tell you what," she said suddenly, far paler than usual. "You can let him out whenever we're not around, but only on one condition."

Stunned by her mother's unexpected change of heart, Dasia stared up at Mrs. Dulane with a reluctant sense of hope. "Of course! Whatever you want," she said before eagerly holding her breath.

Several seconds of tense hesitation followed as Mrs. Dulane glanced over at the frost-covered door. "If anyone ever sees him, or if anyone even suspects that he's here, then we will have no choice but to end his miserable existence once and for all."

"You mean ... you'd actually *kill* your own son?"

"*That* is not our son," Mrs. Dulane said firmly.

"Then what *is* he?" Dasia demanded.

"A tragic mistake your father and I never should've made, and the greatest threat to this family there could possibly be. If anyone ever found out he was here, let alone what we've done to him, then the Asterguards would come and take you both away, and we would never see you again. His very existence is just that dangerous."

Dasia shook her head as she stared down at the floor, a few more tears falling from her pallid cheeks. "Then why didn't you just leave him at the hospital when we were born? Why bring him home and spend all these years just keepin' him locked away?" They were questions Dasia had been dying to ask for as long as she could remember.

"Because the connection between your souls is just too strong," her mother answered with deepest regret. "And because we didn't want to risk leaving yours Broken if we dared destroy his. You are far too precious to us. The beautiful daughter I always wanted, and the very last child I can ever have. So *now* do you understand the position we're in?"

Dasia glanced back at the frost-covered door. "I just want him to be happy," she said desperately.

"He will never be happy. But at least he's still alive. And so are you. Isn't that enough to be grateful for?"

"How could I ever be grateful if he'll spend the rest of his life miserable and alone?"

It was an answer that very nearly broke Mrs. Dulane's heart, though still not enough to make it thaw.

"You know my terms, Dasia," she coldly replied. "No one can ever know he exists, and your father and I don't ever want to see him or even suspect you've let him out. Otherwise, we'll do whatever it takes to end his suffering for good. Now, do we have a deal?" And with those fateful words, Mrs. Dulane held out one hand toward her daughter and nervously awaited her reply.

In the midst of a deafening silence, Dasia turned back toward her mother once more. "He's my brother," she said proudly. "I'll do anythin' for him." And without another moment's hesitation, she grabbed ahold of her mother's forearm, sealing the deal between their souls.

IN THE WEEKS that followed, Dasia anxiously awaited her first opportunity to set Dustane free, even if only for a few brief moments. But with the prolonged injustice that was her parents' lives in Marshwood finally behind them, Mr. and Mrs. Dulane spent every waking moment preparing their new home for its first big celebration—a housewarming party so incredibly grand that it would cement their rightful place as full-fledged members of the Selyrian upper class.

Nearly a dozen laborers and one particularly uptight planner descended upon the Dulane family home in the hours leading up to the big event, leaving Dasia and Demitris confined to their rooms—the only way their parents could ensure they would in no way interfere.

"Everything must be perfect," Mrs. Dulane had insisted, "which means you two better not cause any trouble before tonight is through."

A sparkling violet dress had been laid out on Dasia's bed first thing that morning, right before her parents took their carriage into town. Adorned with crystalline flowers from bodice to hem, the dress was more extravagant than anything Dasia had ever imagined she would wear, and a far cry from the plain mauve frocks she had long been forced to endure.

Yet even as Dasia held the ornate gown up in front of her before the full-length mirror in her room, she could not help but think of the lavish dress as little more than an elaborate costume—one specifically designed to help her parents conceal their greatest lie. Laying the dress back across her bed, Dasia glanced over at the frost-covered door beside the mirror and stared intently at the embossed silver handle. More than anything else, she simply wanted Dustane to partake in the evening's festivities in her place.

It would be so easy to let him out, she told herself. *If I just keep my door shut, no one will ever know.* Then Dasia took a few steps toward the forbidden door, her trembling hand mere inches away from the silver knob. *Maybe just for a few minutes*, she reasoned.

Only then did a subtle whisper finally catch her ear. "Dasia ..."

Dasia froze where she stood, her fingers still lingering near the door. "Dasia ..."

This time she was absolutely certain she had heard her name. And so she began to lean in, inch by inch, until one ear was very nearly pressed against the frozen door's glistening Ildarglass surface.

"Hey!" Demitris shouted, bursting into the room and scaring Dasia half to death. "Didn't you hear me callin'?"

"Argh! Why don't you ever knock when you come in?" Dasia demanded, her heart nearly beating through her chest. "I could've been gettin' dressed."

"Oh, please. You always lock the door when you're changin', so quit bein' so dramatic. Besides, I was hopin' you might wanna help me play a little prank on Mom and Dad."

"Have you lost your mind? They'll kill us!"

"Come on, it's just a harmless little joke. And I promise, they'll have no idea we even had anythin' to do with it."

Dasia took a moment to consider the tempting request. She had always found it difficult to refuse her older brother's invitations for shared mischief. After all, he was more than just her only real friend—he was also the only one to defend her on those rare occasions when she dared speak up on Dustane's behalf.

"Okay, fine. But if we get caught, I'm blamin' whatever it is entirely on you."

"Consider it a deal," Demitris said with a grin.

From the serenity of Dasia's room, the two young Dulanes made their way out into the second-floor hall, which overlooked a seemingly endless flow of commotion in the main entrance hall down below. Making sure to avoid being spotted by any of the hired help, Dasia and Demitris tiptoed down one of the twin spiral staircases before swiftly taking cover behind the family's sparkling new Ildarwood tree.

With jagged, mirrorlike bark and silver leaves made of spectral glass, the Shimmerwood tree had grown thick and tall in just a matter of weeks thanks to extra care and feeding from Mr. and Mrs. Dulane. Prized by the two for its unmatched beauty, it possessed a unique and incredible gift—the ability to show all who gazed into its infinite facets the exact reflection of themselves that they most desperately wanted to see. However, for reasons beyond Dasia's understanding, whenever she tried to catch a glimpse of her own reflection, the crystalline bark did not show her at all—an experience she found most unnerving, to say the least.

"Come on. It looks like they're all headin' back outside to eat lunch," Demitris whispered before hurrying across the hall and into the parlor with his little sister close behind.

Never before had Dasia seen a room so exquisitely appointed as the one she saw that afternoon, with furniture they did not even own carefully placed everywhere she looked, and a dozen varieties of flowers arranged in ornate vases here and there.

"Do people really live in houses that look like this?" she asked with astonishment, suddenly fearful of touching anything but the floor.

"I'm sure *some* people do, but I doubt Mom and Dad can afford it. They said they've spent every last Starling they had just tryin' to put on a good show for tonight."

"So what was your brilliant idea for a prank?" Dasia asked nervously, her eyes perpetually searching for any subtle signs that they might get caught.

"Come over here, and I'll show you." Demitris wasted little time approaching a nearby arrangement of flowers, which rested peacefully in an expensive-looking vase. "Wanna see somethin' cool?"

Dasia hesitated for a moment but could not restrain an eager grin.

"Then watch this." A deep breath followed as Demitris closed his eyes and held out one hand until it was barely an inch away from the closest flowers.

Seconds passed as Dasia grew increasingly impatient, while Demitris, beside her, focused harder and harder in a desperate attempt to impress his little sister. Yet only once she was about to speak up did Dasia finally notice the subtlest twinkle in the air between her brother's hand and the flowers. Staring with amazement, Dasia spotted another twinkle, then several more. And within a minute, an almost invisible stream of spectral energy had begun to flow directly from the flowers into her brother's open palm.

"Is that what I think it is?" asked Dasia, her eyes wide with wonder.

"Yep! It's pure Silver," Demitris replied. "That's what they put in Ildarglass coins to make money, and what every soul needs to stay alive. I *finally* figured out how to control it, just like Mom and Dad. There's just one little problem ..."

Dasia gasped as several of the flowers withered and crumbled right before her eyes. "You killed 'em," she said with surprise, her gaze lingering upon the fallen petals on the table in front of her.

"Well, technically, whoever cut 'em killed 'em. I just took whatever Silver they had left. I've been tryin' to learn how to push Silver *into* stuff too, just like Mom and Dad did to make that new Ildarwood tree grow, but ... well, I haven't quite figured that part out yet. I guess it's a whole lot easier to steal Silver than it is to give it away."

Dasia stood stunned by the demonstration. "You think you could teach me how to do that?" she asked with excitement. But the sudden look of surprise on her brother's face made it abundantly clear that their time had run out.

"They're home!" he announced before ducking suddenly, leaving Dasia standing frozen beside him. Only after a momentary delay did he finally reach up and pull her down to join him.

Raising her head only enough to glimpse out through the parlor's front window, Dasia watched as a pristine new carriage came to an abrupt stop in front of the house. Pulled by two mighty Ildarhorse steeds, which were composed entirely of Ildarwood roots and vines all expertly intertwined, the impressive carriage was yet another temporary acquisition—one which Dasia's parents would most certainly use to further impress their guests that night.

Within seconds, a wave of laborers had hurried into the house and hastily resumed their assigned tasks. But right before Dasia and Demitris could make their covert escape, a single laborer wandered in and found them hiding.

Stopping suddenly, the woman stared down at the two mischievous children with a slightly cocked head, then turned her attention toward the vase of partially shriveled flowers. Her mouth fell open, but she did not speak.

For several agonizing moments, Dasia stared up into the woman's vacant eyes. Like all other people Dasia had met who were Broken, the woman had no visible rings of any color around her pupils—just two lonely black dots, the telltale sign that someone's soul had been entirely shattered by some tragic event in their past.

Demitris raised a single finger up to his lips to plead for silence. Then he retreated with Dasia ever so slowly until they finally reached the home's back door. Only once there were they free to escape out into the frigid cold beyond. And they did not stop running until they reached the safety of the greenwood forest on the other side of their frost-covered lawn.

"Well, that was close," Demitris said with relief, his back pressed against the bark of an ancient elm tree.

"What about that poor Broken woman? Won't she just tell on us, or end up gettin' in trouble herself?"

"First of all, the Broken almost never speak, so I doubt she'd actually tell on us," Demitris reasoned. "And second of all, Mom and Dad told that snooty old planner to make sure everythin' was absolutely perfect before they got back, so they'll probably just end up yellin' at her instead. And based on how mean she's been to all her helpers today, I'm pretty sure she actually deserves it."

Finding some relief in her brother's logic, Dasia finally allowed herself to take a breath. "How long do you think it'll take Mom to notice?" she asked nervously.

An instant later, a soul-piercing shriek exploded through the tranquility of the forest, causing nearby birds to flee and several Ildarglass windows around the house to swiftly shatter.

"About that long," Demitris replied.

A savage barrage of insults and swears swiftly followed as Mrs.

Dulane unleashed her rage upon the pompous planner, leaving Dasia and Demitris to laugh in a secret celebration of their success. Then together they watched as light flurries began to fall upon the vast frozen reaches of Lake Abalus, just beyond the forest's edge.

Only after an hour did they risk returning to the house, where Mr. Dulane anxiously urged them both to get dressed—preferably *before* being spotted by Mrs. Dulane. And no sooner had they finished than they found themselves immediately whisked away by their mother and carefully positioned on either side of the family's wondrous Shimmerwood tree.

"Now, remember what I told you," Mrs. Dulane insisted in a panic. "Be polite. Introduce yourselves to each guest. Be charming. Make sure they really love us. And whatever you do, do *not* embarrass us, or I swear to the Heavens, it'll be the last thing you two ever do."

"Love you too, Mom," Demitris mumbled, forcing Dasia to conceal a sudden laugh. She could always count on her beloved older brother to lift her spirits, even when times were especially tough.

What followed was a night unlike any Dasia had ever imagined, with wave after wave of affluent guests pouring in, each one somehow even more impressive to behold than the last. Every man Dasia met was dressed in nothing less than a well-tailored suit. And never to be outdone, all the women had tightly cinched themselves into a veritable bouquet of glamorous gowns, each of which had been adorned with countless glimmering crystals to catch the eye. Accessorized with dazzling necklaces, earrings, and bangles galore, every lady that night wore a face so unnaturally beautiful that Dasia could not help but feel uncomfortable each time one approached her to speak.

Yet two other peculiar things did each guest have in common, Dasia noticed, both of which caught her entirely by surprise. The first was a small, sparkling piece of white jewelry, which precisely resembled the elaborate eight-point star carefully crafted into the door in Dasia's room. And the second was each guest's utter fascination with the sight of their own reflection in the Shimmerwood tree's mirrorlike bark. In fact, so prolonged were their stares that Mr. and Mrs. Dulane needed to repeatedly escort large groups away to make room for the next.

The housewarming continued for hours once the last of the Dulane family's guests had finally arrived, giving Dasia and Demitris plenty of time to wander about the first floor and listen discreetly to an array of conversations. And though most involved topics that were of no interest to either of them, every now and again, they would overhear one small bit of juicy gossip or another before being noticed.

"I think you two have stayed up long enough," Mrs. Dulane insisted after catching them in the act for the third time. "Why don't you head off to bed? I'll come up to check on you once everyone's gone."

Relieved beyond words that they were both finally free, Dasia and Demitris hurried up the stairs and into their respective rooms. Their long, agonizing night was over at last.

Eager to free herself from the confines of what had turned out to be an elegant cage made from expensive fabrics and sharp wires, Dasia approached the full-length mirror on the other side of her room and stared at her reflection one last time.

I don't even look like me, Dasia thought, utterly perplexed by her parents' insistence upon presenting fake versions of themselves to an entire houseful of complete strangers.

That was when a familiar voice broke the stillness of her room.

"Please let me out."

Dasia glanced at the frost-covered door mere feet away. "I really wish I could," she whispered.

In the silence that followed, Dasia escaped from her elaborate dress at last, then swiftly prepared herself for bed. All she wanted after such an exhausting evening was a peaceful night's sleep.

She had no way of knowing what would happen after her mother's fancy new clocks released a single lonely chime in the middle of the night.

"… *Dasia* …"

The faintest whisper, carried upon the air ever so gently, stirred her awake. She looked around in the darkness, but there was no one else present to be found.

"… *Dasia* …"

One more whisper in the night. Staring at the frost-covered door across the room, Dasia waited until she heard her name again.

"… *Dasia* …"

Only then was she certain. The voice was not coming from within her room but instead from somewhere beyond her closed bedroom door.

Sneaking carefully out into the hall, Dasia was surprised to find the house barely lit, with nearly all candles in the main foyer extinguished. Left with little more than the ambient light of the family's silver Ildarstar to reveal her presence, she proceeded with utmost caution down the nearest spiral staircase in discreet pursuit of whoever had repeatedly spoken her name.

"There are treatments, of course," said an older man, who had found a seat opposite Mr. and Mrs. Dulane in the family parlor. Holding a full glass of amberberry ale, the mustachioed gentleman was turned away from the main archway leading into the room, making it easy for Dasia to watch him without any real fear of being seen. "But most Selyrian Healers would never agree to perform them. No, they all seem perfectly content to let these unnatural creatures continue to exist, but all that does is spread their condition to others like some sort of vile contagion."

"We couldn't agree more," Mr. Dulane replied. "That's why we were so eager to speak with you. From what we've heard, you've performed the procedure hundreds of times before and never had any problems."

"Amberdale is a very special community, as you've no doubt come to learn. Our unwavering faith in the Heavens is the main reason why we survived the Astyrian occupation relatively intact, and that same commitment to spiritual purity is something we look for in everyone who works in the service of this town."

"That's very reassuring," said Mrs. Dulane. "And you can guarantee discretion?"

"Absolutely. No one ever has to know aside from the three of us, and perhaps one or two close colleagues who can offer help along the way. They'll be the ones who make sure the certificate of birth back in Marshwood is discreetly corrected once every last remnant of the boy is finally gone."

"What about Dasia? Will she be hurt?" Mrs. Dulane asked nervously, leaving her daughter with a painful knot in the pit of her stomach.

"I'd have to examine her more closely to be certain. But in most cases, I've been able to eliminate all traces of the imperfect soul without causing any *real* harm to the other."

An audible gasp suddenly escaped from Dasia's mouth.

"What was that?" Mr. Dulane asked suddenly, leaving a dire silence lingering in the cold midnight air.

"Why don't I go check on the kids before we continue?" Mrs. Dulane replied.

Never before had Dasia run so quickly, bounding up the stairs as quietly as she possibly could before racing across the second floor and carefully closing her bedroom door behind her.

Desperation and fear left her sick to her stomach, while immeasurable panic had nearly caused her broken heart to burst right through her chest. She did not know what to do, and she had never before felt quite so helpless.

But then her gaze found its way over to the frost-covered door. Staring at it as tears filled her eyes, she knew she had run out of options. The time had finally come. She needed to set Dustane free before it was too late.

After locking her bedroom door with little more than a thought, she ran across the room and grabbed ahold of the ornate silver doorknob that kept her beloved brother locked away. Yet no matter how hard she pulled or how much she tried to turn it, her desire to set Dustane free was no match for her parents' relentless will to maintain his confinement.

"Dasia, are you in there?" Mrs. Dulane asked as she struggled to open the bedroom door. "Why won't this rotten thing unlock?"

"Dustane?" Dasia whispered urgently. "I'm tryin' to let you out, but I really need your help. Can you *please* help me open the door?"

"Dasia?" Mrs. Dulane called out more urgently after knocking three times. "Dasia, can you please wake up and unlock the door?"

"Dustane, please! I'm beggin' you. You need to wake up and leave right now, before it's too late." Yet only once enough of her sparkling tears had fallen upon the floor did the doorknob finally grow cold and begin to move all on its own.

Releasing it with surprise, Dasia watched as it turned ever so slowly before a telltale click rang out. An instant later, the door swung open, revealing naught but darkness beyond.

"Dustane?" Dasia asked nervously, walking into the shadows even as her mother's knocks and pleas grew louder. "Dustane, are you in here?"

The last thing Dasia could remember seeing was a glowing pair of pale blue eyes staring back at her. Then a surge of ice-cold air filled the room, leaving Dasia paralyzed with fear as an all-consuming darkness suddenly clouded her waking thoughts.

And by the time Dasia had finally regained consciousness the next morning, there was no escaping the soul-crushing consequences of what she had done. Her worst nightmare had come true, and Dustane and Demitris were both gone.

A Time After the Fall

❧ I ❧

An Interrupted Slumber

S O THAT'S HIM? That's the boy who tried to burn down all those houses? I don't suppose he actually told you his name?"

"He didn't have to," replied a pallid man in Ildarglass armor, his cold blue eyes staring through a narrow window into the darkened cell beyond. "He's been here before, and his name is Tannus Ambers."

The dark-skinned woman beside him gasped, one hand swiftly covering her aching heart. "The poor thing," she managed, her gaze lingering upon the sleeping child. "I suppose we shouldn't be surprised after everything that's happened to him, but at least now it all makes sense. Were you able to catch him in the act?"

"Not exactly," the Asterguard replied. "His foster parents sent word that he ran away in the middle of the night. Then one of our patrols found him down near the river."

"Let me guess. He was trying to make a break for the Ildarwood."

"That's certainly the way it looks. And we didn't need to question him for long to figure out why. Apparently, his foster parents were starting to suspect he'd been sneaking out in the middle of the night, but they only confronted him about it last night."

"Then I suppose it's safe to assume they don't want to risk taking him back."

"Not with such young kids of their own to worry about at home. I don't think they're afraid of him hurting them on purpose, of course. I think they're just concerned about what might happen if he gets upset. And all things considered, I can't really say I blame them."

"Unfortunately, neither can I," the woman said with a sigh. "After what he's been through in the past year, he must be struggling with all sorts of difficult emotions, and I can't imagine any foster family in the city would be well suited to taking him in now, even if one actually *was* willing."

"Then what do you want us to do with him? We can't exactly keep an eleven-year-old kid locked up in here forever."

"Nor would any reasonable person ever ask you to. No, I'm afraid we only have two options here, and I suspect he's not going to like either one." Then the woman took a deep breath before approaching the frost-covered door of the cell. Far too many times had she been forced to endure the unnatural cold she would once again experience within.

"Are you *sure* you don't want me to go in there with you?" asked the Asterguard, one hand instinctively finding the hilt of his Ildarglass sword.

"That won't be necessary. I've had to deal with more than a few feisty young men in my day, and I doubt this one even remotely compares to the worst."

When she stepped into the room at last, the woman shuddered as a surge of frigid air rushed to greet her. Bearing the familiar sting of spectral frost, it was a cold so uniquely piercing that it could drain every last ounce of energy from a person's soul while the warmth of their body barely changed. But uncomfortable though the conditions were, the woman knew that such measures were often required when dealing with someone whose blood so brazenly overflowed with spectral fire.

"Good morning, Tannus," the woman said warmly, causing the

shivering blond boy to stir from his exhausted slumber. "I hear you had quite the night."

"Who are *you* supposed to be?" Tannus asked with annoyance, still frustrated beyond measure that his attempt to escape had landed him in jail.

"My name is Nenika Osei, and I'm the Overseer of Trials for this city. Now, I know you're not *technically* old enough to fall under my jurisdiction, but the Asterguards who brought you here thought I may be able to help you nonetheless."

"Help me with what?" asked Tannus, his whole body trembling beneath several thick blankets.

"I'm afraid the family you've been staying with has decided to rescind your invitation, so the city will need to find you somewhere else to live until it's time to start your Trials."

"Great," Tannus grumbled. "So what are my options?"

"The first, and my personal recommendation, is living with your grandmother in Ranewood. As your closest able relative—"

"Nuh-uh, no way," Tannus insisted, shaking his head emphatically as he spoke. "She's cheap and grumpy, and her whole house smells like old soup."

"Well, I'm not sure you'll find the alternative much better," Nenika replied. "You see, the city has no shortage of children with potentially dangerous gifts, such as yours. So whenever we encounter one who might pose a threat, either to others or themselves, we are often required to send them to a special type of Silverward—one where they can receive the *precise* help they need to eventually thrive. The closest one is called Caelum's Keep. It's just a few miles away from here, and it happens to be a facility where I once had the privilege of working. But while such places provide a uniquely critical role in helping children like you to lead normal, happy lives, I suspect you'd find the conditions there only slightly more comfortable than, well ... a room like this."

A moment of silence followed as Tannus studied the Overseer's face, his silver eyes searching for any subtle signs of deception. "You're just tryin' to scare me into livin' with my gram."

Nenika could not help but smirk as she leaned innocently against the frozen cell wall. "If I was *really* trying to scare you, Tannus, you'd know it."

"Oh yeah?" Tannus said with a contemptuous huff. "I'd love to see you try."

Only two simple words did Nenika Osei need to utter in response. *"Faire sombre."* An instant later, all the radiant crystals in the room faded into darkness, leaving only a pair of bright red eyes in their wake.

"You might think you've had a difficult life so far," Nenika said sternly, "but even the worst of your experiences would pale in comparison to all the dangers that await within those woods."

Suddenly, swirls of light began to race through an endless oblivion, until Tannus inexplicably found himself seated beneath a star-filled sky somewhere deep inside the Ildarwood. And so incredibly realistic was the Overseer's illusion that Tannus could hear tiny frogs chirping in their swamp as a cool spring breeze flowed ever so gently through his hair. But the serenity of the scene lasted only for a moment, for the more Nenika spoke, the more terrifying the illusion grew.

"In the darkest corners of the Ildarwood, monsters unlike anything you could possibly imagine hunt helpless souls to feed upon their pain, while vile spirits search relentlessly for any new victims they can freely torment. Sometimes even the trees themselves will turn upon you, binding you so very tightly with their roots that you will be left struggling to breathe.

"But by far the most vicious creatures of all in those woods are called Cynders—the corrupted remnants of Ildarbound children who were simply too weak to finish their Trials. Fueled by fear and an insatiable thirst for the agony of their prey, they stalk the innocent without relent before unleashing immeasurable suffering upon whomever they can catch, all just to bathe in the intoxicating reward that is their precious Silverblood."

Surrounded by a ring of spectral flames, Tannus stood helpless as faceless figures in tattered cloaks danced and laughed all around him. Even closing his eyes failed to stop the terrifying images swirling relentlessly inside his head.

A merciful end only came when the illusion vanished just as abruptly as it had started, leaving Tannus seated once more inside his cell.

"At the end of the day, the decision is yours and yours alone," Nenika told him. "But if I were you, I'd choose family. Ranewood is a far safer place than Silvermarsh these days, especially out in those woods. And I have to imagine that anyone would find a warm and loving home far more comfortable than a place like this. So what will it be?"

Shivering beneath his blankets, Tannus stared up at the imposing woman and considered his options. "Okay, fine," he conceded. "Just promise you'll never make me sit through anythin' like that ever again."

Nenika smiled warmly. "Consider it a deal."

AN ARMORED CARRIAGE awaited Tannus that afternoon as he was escorted outside by Nenika. Constructed from a type of shimmering blue Ildarwood that left a ghostly mist in the otherwise mild winter air, the imposing transport was attached to two massive Ildarhorse steeds, each one with a cold sapphire glow.

"Any chance we can ride in somethin' just a little bit warmer?" Tannus asked, still exhausted from his long night in a frozen cell.

"The Asterguards never take chances with prisoners or runaways, let alone this close to the Ildarwood. That forest has a way of making otherwise reasonable people do impulsive things, especially if they're desperate, and we've already seen what you're capable of. Not many boys your age can summon enough Goldenfire from their souls to nearly burn down a house, so the Frostwater flowing throughout that carriage will help you maintain a state of balance till we get to your new home. After that, what happens will be entirely up to you."

"Great. Can't wait," Tannus grumbled before finally stepping up into the carriage and sitting across from the Asterguard within.

An hours-long ride followed, taking Tannus through the impoverished neighborhoods of Silvermarsh and out into the rural fields and greenwood hills just beyond the ancient city walls. Yet despite the setting's idyllic beauty, Tannus found it impossible to enjoy the scenery, thanks in no small part to the endless potholes and mountain-like bumps the carriage hit continuously along the way.

He never expected that all to change the moment they crossed over a long greenwood bridge. Finding the ride suddenly smooth and enjoyable, Tannus stared up at Nenika in disbelief.

"I think you'll find Ranewood a very different town from the one you're used to," she said with a smirk. "There were no riots here, and most of these people try to take good care of each other. It's not without problems of its own, of course, but you'll be much safer here, and I'd like to think a great deal happier too."

"Would *you* be happy livin' with *your* gram?" Tannus countered, fully expecting to catch Nenika off guard.

"My grandmother lives in a castle all the way back in Ondala, and she spends most of her days reading quietly in a tropical garden that was planted over a thousand years ago by our ancestors. So to answer your question, yes. I would very much love to go live with her, even if only for a year."

A sour expression swiftly emerged on the face of Tannus, who had never been particularly fond of being outsmarted—least of all by an adult. "Then maybe we should *both* go live with her," he grumbled. "It sure sounds a whole lot better than some musty old cottage."

"You'll never find happiness in life if you only ever compare what you have to what you don't," Nenika said sternly. "Perhaps instead, you should just consider being grateful that things aren't worse. After all, there may very well come a day when you lose what little you've got. And if that happens, you'll no doubt be amazed at how very much you miss the way things were before."

"I already do," Tannus somberly replied. And no matter how hard he tried, he still could not fully understand how his life could have possibly taken such a terrible turn in just one short year. Gone were the days of large, sumptuous meals, lovingly prepared by an adoring mother. Gone were the nights of quality time in a cozy woodcraft shop with a well-respected father. Somehow all that remained of his former life was his memories.

Staring longingly out the carriage window, he found his gaze drawn immediately to the last few golden leaves sparkling brightly in the distant Ildarwood forest. Like glimmers of hope left floating in a cold and colorless sea of bleak surrender, the leaves were surrounded by seemingly endless waves of silver-blue Ildarglass, which rose and fell amidst the barren branches of giant greenwood trees and the stark viridian peaks of stubborn pines.

One day, Tannus told himself once the carriage abruptly turned a sharp corner, causing the fabled forest to fade from view. *One day, I'll finally be free.*

The rest of the ride felt interminable to Tannus, tightening a knot in his stomach with each passing moment. Not for a year had he seen his estranged grandmother—a woman so cantankerous in nature that her own son had dreaded the very thought of paying her a visit. "She can't cook. She never stops complaining," Tannus could recall his father saying each winter before their annual holiday trip. "And every single time I set foot in her house, I end up breaking out in hives!"

But even though two years had passed since his last visit to Ranewood, Tannus could still remember every last detail of his gram's old cottage. How small and dated it was compared to his childhood home. How rotten it smelled, even after leaving the windows and doors open for hours on end. But perhaps its most depressing feature, in Tannus's mind, was the frail and crumbling Ildarwood tree that grew in the center of the house. Like some sickly little sapling forever teetering on the verge of collapse, it only ever reminded Tannus of how very close to death his ancient gram was herself.

"Ah, I think we've finally arrived," Nenika announced suddenly, causing Tannus to cringe as the carriage slowed to a stop.

"Is it too late to change my mind?" he asked nervously.

"You made the right choice by coming here," Nenika insisted. "Now you just need to find the strength and courage to see it through."

"But what if I don't like it here?"

Smiling gently in response, Nenika reached into her pocket and retrieved a small card. "Do you know what this is?" she asked before handing it over.

Staring down at the firm piece of paper, Tannus found the words *Mrs. Nenika Osei, Overseer of Trials, Silvermarsh City* emblazoned upon it in sparkling silver ink. "It looks like a callin' card," he replied.

"Indeed it is. Which means that if things ever truly become unbearable here, or if you just need someone to talk to, all you need to do is whisper a message into this, and I promise I'll come back. Okay?"

"Okay," Tannus mumbled.

"Good," Nenika said softly before finally opening the carriage door. "Now, after you."

As Tannus watched the Asterguard step outside first, he knew that the inevitable could be delayed no longer. And so he emerged into the bright midday sun before glancing up at the man in Ildarglass armor. There was nothing Tannus wanted to do more in that moment than flee.

"You're doing the right thing, kid," the Asterguard offered with a nod. "Just try to make the best of it."

"Easy for you to say," Tannus replied. "You've never had to eat my gram's gross cookin'."

A momentary chuckle from Nenika and the Asterguard followed before they proceeded to escort Tannus directly up to the cottage.

Knock, knock, knock. Nenika rapped her knuckles against the moss-covered Ildarwood door. Nothing but silence immediately followed.

"Perhaps she didn't hear us," Nenika said with surprise. But before she could even raise her hand to knock again, the door flew open, and a short old woman stood defiantly within.

"Of course I heard you. I'm old, not deaf," Gram grumbled. "But whatever you two are sellin', I don't want any."

"I assure you we're not selling anything," Nenika swiftly replied. "My name is Nenika Osei, and I've brought your grandson, Tannus, to come live with you."

"Oh, well, in that case, I *definitely* don't want any. So, have a nice day."

"Very funny, Gram," Tannus called out from behind Nenika. "Now, can we *please* just go in and get this over with?"

"Okay, fine, but only if you promise not to burn the place down while we've got company. I just spent all mornin' cleanin'."

Tannus waited until the old woman's back was turned before staring up at Nenika and the Asterguard both with an expression of utter exhaustion. "*Now* do you see why I don't wanna live here?"

Smiles of amusement from his two escorts followed before Nenika gently nudged Tannus in through the door.

Shaking his head with disappointment, Tannus was dismayed to find his new home every bit as tiny and rundown as he had remembered, with thick layers of dust on every surface and barely enough room to walk around the antique couch opposite the fire. In the kitchen stood a worn-out table with three chairs, as well as a broken fourth chair left to linger in the corner. Two small bedrooms could Tannus see in the back—both barely larger than closets. And there, in the center of it all, was the most emaciated Ildarwood tree that Tannus had ever seen—only five feet tall, with pitted bark like tarnished brass and a pitiful Ildarstar burning overhead with barely any life left in it.

"We very much appreciate your being willing to see us on such short ,notice," said Nenika. "As I'm sure you can imagine, we didn't want to force someone as young as Tannus to remain in a holding cell at the Astercourt for any longer than necessary."

"To be honest, I still can't believe you people don't wanna *keep* him locked up," Gram replied before taking a seat at the kitchen table. "Back in my day, spectral arson was just as much of a crime as any other. So maybe one of you can help me understand why my grandson is gettin' special treatment instead of just bein' sent to one of those special places, like Caelum's Keep."

"Great to see you too, Gram," Tannus grumbled, reminded once more of why his father had always hated to visit.

"Well, now, I didn't say I'm not happy to see ya, Tannus, but even the nicest grandmothers in the world are gonna get upset if their families only ever stop by when they're lookin' for presents or parole."

"In this case, the Captain of the Guard decided to show leniency on account of your grandson's *unique* circumstances," said the Asterguard. "Most of the houses he attacked suffered minimal damage, and all the people who owned them were involved in the incident that almost killed him last year. So all things considered, bringing him to live with you seemed like the least drastic course of action we could take."

"Lucky me," Gram replied before glancing over at Tannus. "My only grandson, and he turns out to be a criminal. And not even a good one at that. You're just lucky that rotten father of yours decided to use your mother's last name instead of mine. Heavens forbid people ever found out that someone with my blood wasn't able to start a decent fire."

A look of utter astonishment froze upon Tannus's face before Nenika finally chimed in once more. "Am I correct in understanding that you're willing to take Tannus in and keep him out of trouble until he's old enough to start his Trials?"

"Well, I'm certainly willin' to take him in. It's the keepin'-him-out-of-trouble part I'm worried about."

"I won't be causin' any more trouble," Tannus insisted, his head lowered in defeat.

"I'm glad to hear it. Last thing I need is another headache like your father runnin' around. But don't think I'm too old to spank that flat little butt of yours if you go and step outta line, 'cause I'm not."

Never before had Tannus been quite so eager to die from embarrassment.

"WELL, I SUPPOSE you'll be needin' a place to sleep," Gram announced later that day, just as soon as both her guests were finally gone. Hobbling over to one of the narrow bedrooms, she explained, "This one here was your father's. It's even still got some of his old stuff in it, but you can feel free to toss it all out or even burn it, supposin' you can figure out how."

Choosing to ignore his gram's latest attempt at humor, Tannus approached a part of the wall left blackened by some spectral fire long ago. "What happened here?" he asked while running his fingers along the remnant soot.

"Your father did that one night when he got into a big ole fight with your grampy. That was his last night under this roof. They both ended up sayin' some things they probably regretted—at least, your grampy sure did—and the two never quite saw eye to eye again after that."

"But this wall is made of Ildarwood. Shouldn't it have fixed itself by now?"

"Some scars never heal, no matter how long it's been. And that's probably for the best. More often than not, they're a darn good reminder of things that never should've happened, and they help us make sure they'll never happen again. I suppose you've got more than a few of those yourself by now, especially after everythin' that happened."

Tannus shook his head ever so slightly in response. "I only ended up with a few small cuts and bruises."

"Those aren't the kind of scars I'm talkin' about, Tannus. Some of the worst scars a person can get are the ones most people can't even see. At least, not unless they actually know how to look."

Unsettled by his gram's lingering stare, Tannus turned his attention toward the freshly-made bed, which was barely wide enough to sleep a single person. "I should probably get some sleep. It was a long night."

"I'll bet," Gram replied. "While you're doin' that, I'll go diggin' in the icebox for somethin' I can start on for dinner."

"Hey, Gram," Tannus called out after a moment, causing her to turn back toward him. "Can you at least *try* to make somethin' that actually tastes good?"

A sincere response came swiftly. "I know just the thing," Gram said with a smile. "In fact, your grampy once said it was the best meal I ever made him. Of course, he died right after eatin' it, but I'm pretty sure my cookin' had nothin' to do with that. Now, sleep well!"

Needless to say, he did not.

"RISE AND SHINE, Tannus!"

It had been the exact same greeting morning after morning for weeks on end. And nearly every time, those four dreaded words were followed immediately by a blinding stream of golden daylight, which surged in mercilessly through his bedroom door.

"How can you possibly be so awake this early?" Tannus asked with annoyance just a few days shy of the new year.

"Years of practice! Now hurry up and get movin'. You've got a lot of chores to do."

Tannus stirred from his bed with utmost resentment. He hated his gram's morning routine more than anything else in his life. Every day without relent, he was forced to make breakfast for the two of them—assuming he even had any appetite at all. And once they had finished eating, he was expected to clean up every last crumb before spending the rest of the day completing whatever tedious tasks his gram seemed to invent to keep him busy.

"Remind me again why *you* can't do any of this stuff," Tannus said after sweeping the tiny cottage for the third time that week.

"Well, I'd love to blame it on just bein' old and brittle, but I was doin' most of this stuff just fine before you got here. Nope, the real reason I make you do it is 'cause that awful son of mine went and pampered you like a baby, and now I'm the one who's gotta get you ready for a life that's gonna be a whole lot harder than the one you've had so far."

"So ... what? All these chores are just your way of doin' me some sort of favor?"

"You're darn right. And one day or another, I'm sure you'll actually thank me for it. But until that day comes, I'm just gonna keep on sittin' myself down by this nice warm fire and enjoyin' what precious little time I've got left."

Tannus rolled his eyes as he put away the broom. "Well, couldn't you at least help a little bit so it's not *just* me doin' all this stuff? I mean, wouldn't that be way more fair?"

"Oh, I certainly *could* do that. But I won't. Nope, the way I see it, your grampy and I spent our whole lives earnin' just enough Silver to keep us from havin' to starve when we got older, but now what little money I've got left has to take care of you and me both for at least another year. And let me tell you right now, feedin' a growin' boy ain't cheap! So as far as I'm concerned, this right here is your way of pullin' your own weight till you're old enough to start your Trials. And if you ask me, doin' some light chores all day is a small price to pay to have a dry roof over your head in a nice town like this."

Exasperated by the old woman's logic, Tannus abruptly stopped in the middle of the room, then gestured emphatically toward a nearby puddle. "You call that dry?" he asked with annoyance as melting snow dripped down from above.

"Oh, don't look at me like that. I said the *roof* was dry. I didn't say nothin' about the floor. Now hurry up and grab a bucket!"

Such was the way most days went in the weeks after Tannus had left Silvermarsh. Yet even when the heavy snows began to fall, sparing Tannus from his weekly walk into town to buy supplies, he was dismayed to find that his gram had no shortage of arduous tasks for him to perform from dawn to dusk.

Only the thought of the coming holiday was enough to raise his tired spirits, for the sacred night of Ansolas—the annual festival celebrating the last and longest night of the year—was fast approaching. In the past, it had always brought with it delicious meals and heartfelt gifts, even during his short-lived stay with a foster family the year before. But as shorter and shorter days turned into long, frigid nights, Tannus began to suspect that his next Ansolas might not come with very much cause for celebration at all.

"Are you gonna make anythin' special for tonight?" Tannus asked timidly, his last breakfast of the year finally cooked and served. "It looks like the snow isn't as deep as it was a few days ago, so I can go into town to get some fresh food if you want."

His gram sat quietly by the fire as he spoke, her knitting needles working at twice their normal speed. "I really wish we had the money, Tannus," she said after a sigh, "but I'm afraid we just don't. Nope, we'll just have to do somethin' simple tonight, and leave it at that."

"But we're still doin' gifts, right?"

It was a question asked with such desperation that it nearly broke Gram's old heart. "Of course we are," she replied, finally pausing her work. "I just wouldn't get my hopes up if I were you. Your mom and dad used to spoil you somethin' rotten, and I just can't do that sort of thing for ya, nor would I even want to. Nope. The next few years are gonna be tough, especially once you start your Trials, so it's probably best you start gettin' used to makin' do with less. Then, if somethin' good actually *does* come along every now and again, you might just appreciate it a little bit more."

Yet even the news that he would still be getting presents did little to cheer Tannus up, for more than anything else in the world, he just wanted that single night to remind him of better times back home.

Hours passed as darkness descended upon the quiet town of Ranewood, leaving Tannus to find what little comfort he could in his gram's modest attempt at a flavorful holiday meal. Then together they sat on the old couch by the fire, giving Tannus the chance to present the heartfelt gift he had worked on every night for weeks.

Shaped to resemble a blooming desert rose, the small sculpture had been carved out of a stray piece of Ildarwood he had found on the side of the road not far from town. Yet only once Tannus had placed the flower gently into his gram's waiting hands did it begin to release a warm golden glow.

"Oh, Tannus, it's beautiful!" she said through tearful eyes.

"Dad showed me a picture of a flower that looked just like that when I was little. He said it was your favorite, 'cause it reminded you of your family crest."

"Well, I guess it's nice to know he wasn't *entirely* rotten. And I couldn't be more grateful he actually taught you how to do somethin' useful before he went and ruined so many lives. What a waste. There just aren't enough people in the world who can look at somethin' plain and simple, like an old piece of wood, and see somethin' so beautiful just waitin' to come out inside. It's a real gift, Tannus, and you should be very proud."

Tannus smiled widely. He had never expected such a touching

reaction from the woman who seemed so intent on filling his life with endless teasing and chores. Yet as he watched her shed a few sparkling tears, he realized for the very first time how much she genuinely loved him.

"Now, I know you're used to gettin' all sorts of nice things from your parents on a night like this," Gram began before reaching for a small wooden box, "but I hope you can at least understand that this was the best I could do."

Struggling to keep his expectations low, Tannus still found himself overwhelmed with disappointment upon opening the box and finding an assortment of knitted clothing folded neatly inside.

"I'm sorry they're not as fancy as the clothes you used to get," his gram offered, "but I know how much you hate the cold, so I thought these might at least help to keep you warm."

"They're really nice, Gram," Tannus managed, even as his soul cried out for a swift and merciful end to his misery. "Thank you."

"You're very welcome. Now, how'd you like to hear some old stories about Ansolas?"

"Actually, I should probably just head off to bed," Tannus said before standing, his eyes eager to avoid his gram's perceptive gaze. "It's already startin' to snow, and I'm guessin' you'll want me to go out and clear it first thing, so …"

"Oh, okay," Gram replied. "Well, if you change your mind, you know where to find me."

Retiring to his room and closing the door most of the way behind him, Tannus could not shake the feeling of complete and utter defeat that had washed over him. His parents were gone. All his childhood friends were back in Silvermarsh. And though life with his gram was not a complete disaster, the mere thought of having to spend another year taking care of her was almost more than he could bear.

Maybe I would've been better off in Caelum's Keep, Tannus thought, his stare finding the sparkling calling card he had been given by Nenika

Osei. Then he turned his gaze out through his bedroom window into the snowy greenwood forest beyond. Imagining a life of limitless freedom in the Ildarwood, Tannus set aside his fears and all the warnings he had been given about the dangers of the Trials. And for a few magical moments, he even convinced himself that his gram would actually be better off without him.

Such were his final waking thoughts as he crawled into bed and prayed in silence for even one meager chance at a better life. He had only just started to dream when a sudden chill caused him to shiver, head to toe.

Unsettled by the strange sensation, Tannus glanced first at the closed, snow-covered window beside his bed. Then he rolled over to confirm that the golden glow of the fireplace in the living room was still present. Only after glancing down toward the foot of his bed, however, did he notice the pale little boy staring back at him.

Nearly leaping out of his skin, Tannus could not believe what he was seeing. "Fynn?" Tannus whispered with alarm. "I thought you were dead!"

But not a single word did the little boy speak in response.

"How did you even get in here?" Tannus asked desperately. Yet the longer he stared at his old friend, the more evident it became that the boy standing before him was not truly what he seemed.

"You're not really here right now, are you?" Tannus asked as a few fleeting memories of his mother's bedtime stories raced to the forefront of his mind. "I can only see you 'cause it's Ansolas. My mom used to say most spirits can only appear outside the Ildarwood on the longest night of the year, but I always thought she was just makin' that up."

Yet no matter what Tannus said, the boy still did not respond. Instead, the ghostly figure merely walked across the room and stood in front of the only window, his attention focused entirely on the falling snow beyond.

"Fynn?" Tannus asked again.

Then the boy turned to face him one last time before touching the Ildarglass pane with his palm and suddenly vanishing from sight.

"Fynn!" Tannus called out urgently, his voice still low despite the sheer immensity of his alarm. He raced over to the window and stared outside, only to see his long-lost friend shivering helplessly in the merciless winds of a savage blizzard.

Tannus opened the window with urgent haste, then pleaded with the boy to come back inside. But as soon as the words left his mouth, the spirit raced off into the surrounding woods, leaving only a ghostly glow behind.

"Hey! Where are you goin'?"

"Tannus?" Gram called out from the other room. "What in the Heavens' name are you doin' in there with the window open? Are you tryin' to make me freeze to death?"

Unsure of how to answer, Tannus merely glanced back in the direction of her voice. Part of him wanted to warn her. Part of him wanted to flee. But the loudest voice inside his head reminded him once more, *She'd just be better off without you.*

Terrified of losing his friend again, Tannus refused to waste any more time. So he grabbed his only winter cloak from a nearby chair, then leaped into his thickest pair of boots. And utterly convinced that no mere storm could ever stop him, he climbed out into the snow and closed the window firmly behind him.

"I'm sorry," he whispered, one hand pressed against the glass. And just like that, he had resigned himself to whatever dire consequences fate might have in store.

Trudging through two feet of snow as whipping winds left him frigid down to the bone, Tannus fixed his gaze upon the distant light that beckoned him forth like some radiant star in the night. He did not stop for rest. He did not even consider giving up and heading back. All he wanted to do was find his old friend and see him one last time.

Only once the spirit of the boy had raced into the Ildarwood did Tannus finally pause to consider his next steps. Nenika Osei had warned him about the dangers lurking within the ancient forest, yet there he stood, upon its edge, compelled to enter by circumstances he did not fully understand. Desperate to know if it was safe to proceed, he stared into the woods, past the broken fence that might have otherwise blocked his way. Then he spotted his old friend staring back at him. An instant later, the boy turned and ran even deeper into the forest, leaving Tannus to decide whether to continue his midnight pursuit.

Just a single step into the Ildarwood did Tannus take before a wave of dizziness suddenly washed over him. Lasting only for a moment, the strange effect was immediately followed by a deep, unnatural cold even more severe than the frigid jail cell he had endured back in Silvermarsh mere weeks before. Yet even so, he could not resist the urge to chase after his lost friend.

Pushing past briars and brush that had been weighed down by weeks of snow, Tannus found no tracks that he could follow. All he had to guide him was momentary flashes of light that seemed to perpetually define his course. So on he went, past dozens of trees with Ildarglass leaves and all the countless glowing beads that protruded ever so slightly from their crystalline trunks. And he did not stop again until he arrived at last before a scene that left him breathless.

In the center of a small clearing, Tannus found an Ildarwood tree unlike any he had ever seen before. With twin narrow trunks and pale white bark, it had dangling pale blue catkins that resembled frozen tinsel left glowing in the night. Its rounded, glass-like leaves gave off a soothing chime that echoed out into the forest, while all around it, cerulean wisps danced and flickered in the darkness, undeterred by the falling snow.

Taking a few steps forward, Tannus noticed something even more peculiar at its base—a shivering girl with silver-blond hair who had fallen asleep atop the tree's glimmering roots.

"Hey, are you all right?" Tannus asked nervously, pulling aside the girl's gray winter cloak just enough to check her neck for a pulse. Finding only the most fleeting of heartbeats, Tannus feared that she would not survive for long if he decided to leave in search of help.

"You're gonna be okay," he told her, even as the wisps around him moved ever closer. Already weakened by the unnatural cold of his surroundings, Tannus slowly succumbed to the strangely soothing chimes of the Ildarwood tree before him. His final desperate act was to cover the mysterious girl with his cloak and lie beside her—their lingering warmth not nearly enough for either one to survive the night all on their own.

In the moments that followed, a deep and debilitating darkness swiftly consumed his final thoughts, leaving Tannus utterly convinced that neither one of them would ever wake again.

II

A Heart Left Broken

I T WAS THE piercing whistle of a teapot that awakened Dasia Dulane the next morning, though no recollections did she have of being brought inside. Lying upon a musty old mattress in a small room filled with clutter, Dasia glanced in the direction of the Goldenfire flames burning gently in a hearth nearby.

"It's about time you woke up," a weathered old woman announced, entering the room with a large glass of hot tea. "You and your little friend were lucky I found yas when I did."

"My friend?" Dasia asked with surprise, her eyes lighting up for a moment.

"Yep. A skinny blond boy, about your height. Had a little tag in his cloak that said 'Tannus Ambers.' Any chance that rings a bell?"

Dasia's hopes were immediately dashed. "Oh, um … no. I don't think so," she mumbled.

"Not who you were hopin' for, I take it," the old woman said knowingly.

"Not exactly," Dasia replied, her attention drifting to the forest outside. "We're still in the Ildarwood. Does that mean you're one of the teachers out here?"

"We call ourselves Preceptors," the old woman answered with a smile. "And you can call me Etta. I teach all the first-year Ildarbound everythin' they need to know about greenwood trees and Ildarwood trees alike—or at least as much as they're willin' to learn. Now, what would you like me to call *you*?"

A momentary silence followed as Dasia considered her response. The last thing she wanted was to get in trouble for sneaking out in the middle of the night, but the longer she stared into Etta's sparkling silver eyes, the more certain Dasia became that she could trust the friendly old woman. "My name's Anaesdasia, but everyone just calls me Dasia for short."

"Huh, well, isn't that funny? You don't look like a Dasia to me," Etta said with a chuckle. "But even so, it's nice to meet you. Now, why don't you go ahead and drink this? I'm sure it'll help you feel better."

"What is it?" Dasia asked before lifting the glass up to her nose.

"Elyshan sweet tea, although I put a few small emberberries in it to give it a little extra kick. Should warm you right up and get you back on your feet in no time. I know these always do the trick for me."

Finally risking a sip from the steaming glass, Dasia could hardly believe the incredible taste that greeted her lips. Warm and sweet with a strange type of heat that flowed directly into her soul, it was unlike anything she had ever drunk before. And so utterly delicious did she find the flavorful concoction that she very nearly drank the entire glass in a single eager gulp.

"That was amazin'!" she said cheerfully, experiencing genuine joy for the first time in months. "Would it be okay if I had another?"

"No, no. One is more than enough for now. After all, nothin' good ever comes from havin' too much Goldenfire in you. Now, why don't you get a little bit more rest while I go check on your friend?"

"May I come with you?" asked Dasia, her eagerness suddenly so overflowing that she nearly leaped out of her bed.

"Well, sure, if you want. Although it might be a while before he wakes up. Between the cold, the wisps, and that old Slumberwood tree, his spirits are runnin' awful low."

"That's okay," Dasia insisted. "I don't mind sittin' with him for a while."

It was a strange house that Dasia found herself walking through that morning—at once both warm and welcoming, while at the same time feeling sad and forgotten. Thick layers of dirt and grime coated every surface, while piles of various objects littered both sides of the hall. Even the Ildarwood floorboards were covered in years of caked-on dirt from the forest and gardens outside, leaving Dasia to question the overall wellness of Etta herself.

But the most fascinating sight to behold for young Dasia was the massive Ildarwood tree growing up through the center of the house. Though only two stories tall, it had a twisted, knotted trunk that was far thicker than any other Ildarwood tree that Dasia had seen before. Its sparkling bark was jet black, and its long, sprawling branches seemed to endlessly drip water as if perpetually soaked by passing storms.

"What kind of an Ildarwood tree is that?" Dasia asked nervously.

"Oh, just the kind that helps an old lady like me still get through the day." And though Etta smiled gently as she answered, Dasia could sense a certain loneliness in the old woman's response.

Only after walking around the hulking tree could Dasia finally see into the living room, where the mysterious blond boy still lay motionless upon a couch.

"Look familiar?" Etta asked expectantly.

Dasia stared at the boy's face as golden light from the nearby hearth danced upon it. "I don't think so."

"Huh. Then I wonder why he was tryin' to protect you."

"He was?" Dasia asked with astonishment. "But … why would he do that if he's never even met me before?"

Etta grinned as she nudged Dasia toward a nearby chair, directly across from the sleeping boy. "I guess we'll have to ask when he wakes up. Now, why don't you just make yourself comfortable? And I'll go make us some food."

Nodding politely, Dasia reluctantly lowered herself into a musty armchair with worn-out cushions. And for the next few hours, she watched and wondered as the boy across the room twitched and trembled in the flickering light of a spectral fire.

THE MOUTHWATERING SMELL of pan-fried food drifted swiftly into the living room that morning, leaving Dasia longing for the days when her parents had still cared enough to cook her breakfast. Yet she found herself breathless with surprise when the savory aroma caused the sleeping boy to stir at last.

"Mmm, that almost smells like bacon," he mumbled, still too tired to recall all that had transpired the night before.

"I think that's exactly what she's makin'," Dasia nervously replied, entirely unsure of how Tannus would react once fully awake.

"Oh, good. It's about time," he said with a yawn before finally opening his eyes and sitting up with alarm. "What are you doin' in my room?"

"We're not in your room. We're in the Ildarwood," said Dasia, who suddenly grabbed ahold of a dirty old throw pillow for protection. "Don't you remember comin' out here last night?"

Moments passed in silence as Tannus glanced around the room. "I remember seein' a tree … and you … and a bunch of floatin' lights. But … how did we end up here?"

"The Preceptor who lives here found us. Her name's Etta. And mine's Dasia."

The boy stared at her suspiciously before once more studying every last detail of his surroundings. "My name's Tannus. But—"

"Finally! You really had me worried there for a bit," said Etta, who entered the room with a tall glass of tea and two steaming hot plates of sizzling food. "Now, why don't you two go ahead and eat? Hopefully, it'll help you both feel better in no time."

Reluctant to trust the strange old woman, Tannus waited for a friendly nod from Dasia before accepting Etta's generosity.

"How'd you even know where to find us?" Tannus asked between bites. "Did somebody tell you we were lost?"

"Not exactly," Etta replied. "I just like to check on that old Slumberwood tree as often as I can, especially around this time of year. One of the spirits that live there has a nasty little habit of trickin' people into payin' it a visit every year on Ansolas."

"Wait, what do you mean by 'trickin' people'?" Dasia asked with surprise.

"Let's just say you two weren't the first to happen across that particular tree in the middle of the night," Etta said with a somber smile before walking over to the fireplace. "And a long time ago, neither was I."

From atop the mantel, she removed a single picture. Her tearful gaze lingered upon the image for several moments before she finally turned it toward her guests. Only then could they see the lovely young woman whose radiant joy had been so perfectly captured in Ildarglass that Dasia was briefly overcome by it herself.

"This little ray of Elyshan sunshine was called Ambrosia Vale," said Etta. "But we all called her Ambra for short. I first met her durin' my Trials, back when I was, oh, about sixteen years old. And boy, if she wasn't just the sweetest soul I ever did meet."

After turning the picture back toward herself, Etta stared longingly down into the young girl's eyes once more. "I loved her more than anythin' else in the world, and for reasons I still don't quite get, she ended up fallin' in love with me. Of course, in normal times, we would've been free to spend the rest of our lives together, just as soon as our Trials were over, but all those years ago … well, let's just say those weren't normal times.

"You see, back then, this part of Selyria was still overrun by Astyrians, and you may or may not know this, but most Astyrians have certain strong opinions about what sorts of things are okay in the eyes of the Heavens and which ones aren't. Of course, it wasn't enough for them to just live accordin' to their own beliefs, like most of the rest of us do. Nope. They had to make sure everyone else lived by those same rules too.

"That's why Ambra and I had to spend nine whole years livin' apart and leadin' separate lives, all just to keep the Astyrians from hurtin' us or worse. We just couldn't risk anyone findin' out, especially not with so many folks still so eager to try and earn favor with those soldiers—their so-called Astyrgards. Nine whole years. So much time wasted havin' to hide our true selves from the world. So many memories we never had the chance to make. So much loneliness we were both forced to endure. But as some Preceptors like to say, hard times may be inevitable, but then so too are the winds of change. So that's why we both held out hope. For nine whole years."

"That sounds awful," said Dasia, her heart breaking for the old woman. "Did things ever get better?"

Etta shook her head with disappointment as tears began to fall from her sparkling silver eyes. "After all that time, we honestly thought they were about to, since right around then was when the end of the war was finally in sight. But the Astyrians, well … they had a sayin' too … 'Bad things always come upon the ninth.' And sure enough, that ninth year was when their soldiers finally figured out the truth about us."

"So … what happened?" Tannus asked nervously.

"Well, let's just say Astyrians rarely wait to inflict their own cruel forms of justice when given the chance," Etta answered. "I was runnin' an errand for Signora Fiori when it happened. And from what I heard when I got back, a bunch of soldiers showed up to Ambra's house in the middle of the day and took her by force. She put up one heck of a good fight, all things considered, but apparently, there wasn't a single thing she or anyone else could do to stop 'em."

Dasia gasped, while Tannus silently stared into the fire, his face growing stern and bitter as the familiar flames of vengeance ignited deep within his heart.

"I had to go deep into hidin' after that," said Etta, "and I kept hopin' I'd somehow see her again, or at least hear what happened to her. But months went by without so much as a single trace or little whisper, even after the war was finally over. Then at the end of that miserable year came Ansolas ... my first one without her since we'd met ... and boy, if that wasn't one of the hardest nights of my entire life, 'cause I just knew that if I saw her spirit, it'd mean she really was gone, and gone for good. And sure enough, right after midnight ... well, that's when she appeared outside my window ... just as beautiful as ever, with a smile so warm it could melt all the snow in the Ildarwood."

Shimmering tears fell from Etta's cheeks as she continued her story, her trembling eyes focused solely on the woman in the picture. "I should've known it wasn't really her, but I was so desperate to believe it was that I ran outside, only to watch her run off into the woods. I followed her all the way out to the Slumberwood tree that night, and for a few magical moments, I honestly believed we might actually be together forever ..."

Nearly a minute passed in full silence as Etta recalled that terrible night.

"It wasn't really her, was it?" Dasia asked breathlessly, she and Tannus both on the edge of their seats.

"Nope," Etta answered bitterly. "And I almost died because of it.

But then I woke up the next day, beside a fire just like this. Turns out, one of my old Preceptors had found me and brought me all the way back home. And that's when she told me the hard and honest truth. What I really saw that night was somethin' called a Mimicus—a kind of awful, vicious spirit that likes to survive by seekin' out as many desperate souls as it can. That way, it can lure them into dangerous traps and drain their Silver while they suffer."

Shedding a few more tears, Etta placed the picture back upon the mantel before turning to face her guests once more. "My soul ended up Broken after that, and it took me years to recover. Even more years I'll never get back. But part of the fun of livin' a long life is havin' to learn some hard lessons, and if any of the stuff I went through can help keep others from endin' up the same way, then, well … at least I'll know all those years weren't entirely wasted. I guess that's why it's important for kids like you to know my story, 'cause I'd just hate to see those sorts of things happen ever again."

Dasia and Tannus exchanged reluctant glances as another long silence filled the room. They both knew exactly what Etta was going to ask next, yet neither one wanted to confess the truth.

"You both saw spirits last night, didn't you?" Etta asked somberly.

She did not even need them to speak to know the answer, for their sullen expressions alone spoke volumes.

"I'm so sorry," she offered, crouching down just enough to meet them both at eye level as they sat back in their seats and began to sulk.

"I should've known it wasn't real," said Dasia. "I thought all my wishes had finally come true."

"That's what makes a Mimicus so dangerous," said Etta. "And so cruel."

"Then why haven't you killed it?" asked Tannus, his simmering rage finally beginning to show through. He never enjoyed being tricked, let alone in such a cold and heartless way.

"Well, I'd be lyin' if I said I've never tried, but spirits aren't exactly the easiest things to catch, let alone out here. Some of 'em can sense you thinkin' about 'em before you even leave the house, and even if you do somehow manage to sneak up on one, they only need a split second to disappear and show up somewhere else. But boy, would I give anythin' just to make that one go away for good."

Endlessly pained by her aging joints, Etta took a moment to stand before staring down at her guests one last time. "Now, normally, I wouldn't want to pry into who yas saw, or even what the spirits said, but I'm afraid this time I don't have much of a choice. You see, in all the years I've been keepin' an eye on that Slumberwood tree, that awful old spirit has only ever managed to lure out one person at a time. But tonight, well ... obviously, it somehow managed to trick two. So that means either it's gotten a lot more dangerous all by itself, or it's somehow found a friend. And I've really gotta know if it's one of those two or somethin' else. That way, I can figure out what to do next."

"What do you need to know?" Dasia asked reluctantly, terrified by the mere thought of having to reveal such personal details.

"The spirits you thought you saw ... obviously, they were people you loved," Etta began, her glistening eyes finding those of Dasia and Tannus in turn. "And if I had to guess, they must've been people who've passed on. Now, most of the time, the Mimicus I've been dealin' with won't just make itself look like a person you loved, it'll try to sense the deepest and most desperate desires of whoever it wants to trick. That way, it can tell 'em everythin' they wanna hear, then convince 'em to follow it all the way out to that tree."

"But my spirit didn't talk," said Tannus, catching Etta entirely by surprise. "He just appeared in my room and stared at me, all cold and sad, before goin' outside and makin' me chase him out here."

"The person you thought you saw," said Etta, "did you ever talk to him back when he was still around? Do you still remember the sound of his voice and the way he spoke?"

"Yeah, we talked all the time," Tannus answered, perplexed by the old woman's questions. "Why? Is that important?"

"Oh, you could certainly say that," Etta said with relief before walking across the room and taking a seat once more. "You see, here's the thing you need to know about spirits—they all need Silver to survive. That's why everyone calls Silver the 'lifeblood of a soul.' The problem is, pure Silver ain't all that easy to come by, even out here, so most spirits won't waste what little they've got unless they really don't have any other choice."

Leaning forward in her chair, she explained, "One of the first things they'll teach yas out here is that every time a spirit interacts with our world, it has to use up some of its Silver. That's why most of 'em spend what's left of their lives without ever bein' seen or heard again. It takes a lot of Silver for a spirit to show themselves to a person who's awake. It takes a lot more for one of 'em to be heard. And it takes the most for 'em to actually reach out and touch somethin' in the physical world. But the Mimicus usually does all those things. So I guess what I'm tryin' to say is ... maybe the spirit that visited Tannus wasn't a Mimicus after all."

Meeting Etta's stare, Dasia considered the old woman's words before glancing over at Tannus. "You think the spirit he saw was real?" she asked, her gaze finding Etta once more.

"It's entirely possible," said Etta, "but then again, I can't imagine why any normal spirit would want him to risk freezin' to death in all this snow. Unless ..."

"Unless what?" Tannus asked anxiously, his attention darting back and forth between Etta and Dasia both.

"Unless there was a darn good reason for you two to meet," Etta replied.

Dasia and Tannus stared at each other with bewilderment.

"I don't understand. Why would any spirit want him to meet *me*?" Dasia asked timidly, utterly convinced of her limited worth.

"I wish I knew," said Etta. "But for thousands of years, people all over the world have believed that spirits can see glimpses of the future. That's why they sometimes try to find a way to either warn or help those still livin'. And part of our job as Preceptors is to try and interpret all the subtle signs we think we're gettin' from 'em. That way, it's easier for us to guide as many kids as we can safely through their Trials. Only problem is, the signs we get aren't always crystal clear, so sometimes we've just gotta let things play out till we finally understand what the spirits have really been tryin' to say."

Dasia glanced at Tannus once more. She could hardly imagine why any spirits at all would want someone to risk their life to find her, especially after the tragic night she had experienced back in Amberdale the year before.

"So what happens now?" asked Tannus. "Are you gonna send us both back home?"

Dasia gasped at the very thought of returning to her parents, drawing all attention back to her.

"I take it you don't want that to happen," Etta said with newfound concern.

"It's just … my mom and dad don't exactly like me," said Dasia, her heart breaking as the words escaped her lips. "They'd rather pretend I don't exist. And sometimes I can even hear 'em talkin' about how much they're lookin' forward to the day I finally start my Trials. That way, they'll never have to see me again."

"They sound like monsters," said Tannus, his own heart suddenly breaking for the downcast girl sitting across from him.

"They didn't use to be," Dasia said sullenly, several sparkling tears of Silver falling gently onto the dirty old pillow she had begun to hold so very tight.

"I think maybe you two should get a bit more rest while I figure out what to do next," said Etta. "At the very least, the Principal Preceptor out here should know I found you, just in case anyone's out there lookin'."

"They won't be," Dasia said with utmost certainty. "At least, not for me."

NO FURTHER REST came to Dasia that morning, though neither was it found by the anxious boy across the room. Furtive glances between the two came every now and again, each one secretly wondering how the other had been lured out into the Ildarwood in the middle of the night. Neither dared to admit whom they had been so desperate to see when it had happened.

"Well, I've got good news and bad news," Etta announced as she returned from the kitchen, a slender Soundstone held firmly in one hand. "The good news is I just heard back from someone at the Astercourt in town, and Tannus, it sounds like your gram was pretty darn happy to hear you're all right."

Yet even as Dasia watched Tannus exhale with relief, she could not shake the dread that came with sensing what the bad news was about to be. "Let me guess," she began. "My mom and dad didn't even know I was gone."

"It doesn't sound like they did," Etta reluctantly confessed.

But it was the uncomfortable silence that followed that made Dasia realize far worse news was still to come.

"That wasn't the bad news, was it?" she asked timidly, suddenly afraid to hear any more.

"Maybe we should talk somewhere a little more private," Etta suggested, her sideways gaze finding Tannus as he watched on with rapt attention.

"It's okay," Dasia said dejectedly. "He might as well hear it too."

Reluctant to proceed, Etta found herself a seat beside Dasia. "The reason it took me so long to hear back from anyone at the Astercourt was 'cause your mom and dad have officially petitioned the Overseer of Trials to let you stay in the Ildarwood."

The words cut through Dasia's heart like jagged blades made from the world's most merciless spectral ice.

"I'm so sorry," Etta offered, one hand finding Dasia's shoulder to offer some small measure of support.

"So … what happens now?" Dasia dared to wonder as a few fleeting tears cascaded down her face, leaving her spirit nearly shattered and all emotions briefly numbed.

"I'm not really sure," said Etta. "Overseer Brent is gonna review the petition with his wife, who just so happens to be the Principal Preceptor out here. And knowin' Principal Brent, she'll wanna have a word or two with your mom and dad before anythin' is final. But if the petition *is* approved, then, well … we'll have to find you a new home. If not here in Ranewood, then maybe in Silvermarsh or Riverport, or possibly Amberdale, if I had to guess."

Amberdale. Another merciless slash through Dasia's heart. Suddenly, scenes from her worst nightmares began to flash before her eyes, forcing her to relive every ounce of the pain she had endured since the night her entire family had been torn apart.

"Isn't there anythin' you can do to help her?" Tannus asked desperately.

"I really wish there was," said Etta. "But it's outta my hands."

Silence filled the room once more as Dasia crumpled into Etta's arms, leaving Tannus to watch on helplessly.

"Who will come and get us?" he asked after several long moments.

"Well, since neither of you is Ildarbound yet, it'll probably be Asterguards from town. I imagine one of 'em will take you right back to live with your gram. And given the circumstances, I'd like to hope she won't be too mad at you for comin' all the way out here in the middle of the night."

"You don't know my gram," Tannus grumbled, entirely certain of how irate his little adventure would have made the feisty old woman.

A subtle smirk from Etta followed before she turned her attention back to Dasia. "As for you, the Asterguards will probably take you up to Westwatch on the way back to town. That's the closest outpost in these woods, so the Principal Preceptor will meet you there. And what happens after that, well … your guess is as good as mine."

A deep and inescapable loneliness washed over Dasia as she considered her dire fate. No matter how hard she tried, she could not possibly understand how or why she had come to deserve such suffering.

"I think now might be a good time to make you two a bit more tea," Etta offered. "Might not be much, but hopefully, it'll help make yas both feel a little bit better before you go."

Nothin' could ever make me feel better, Dasia silently told herself. *I'll never, ever be happy again.*

Across the room, Tannus watched her intently, his own mind racing to think of something he could say or do to offer comfort. Struggling to find the right words, he decided instead to walk across the room and take a seat at Dasia's side.

"If it makes you feel any better, I had to live with foster parents once," he said softly. "It really wasn't so bad. They were both nice people, and they tried really hard to make sure I was happy in their home."

"So why'd you leave?" asked Dasia, her sparkling eyes finally finding his own.

Reluctant to answer at first, Tannus searched his heart for the truth. "I guess I just didn't really think I deserved it," he said finally. "Not after everythin' I did and all the stuff that got me sent there in the first place."

"Why? What'd you do?" asked Dasia, utterly convinced that nothing Tannus said could possibly compare to her own perceived crimes.

"The spirit I saw last night," said Tannus, "the one who led me all the way out to you …" Yet as the next few soul-crushing words approached his trembling lips, Tannus could not bear to speak them aloud. Entirely convinced that they would become an irrefutable truth once uttered, he had never dared divulge them to anyone. But in that moment, with Dasia staring at him so desperately, they seemed to leap from the end of his tongue all on their own. "I'm the reason he died," he said finally.

It was the first time in over a year that Dasia felt a genuine connection to another living soul. Not only had Tannus chosen to share his deepest, darkest secret, but it just so happened to precisely mirror her own.

"I'm so sorry," she offered, gently taking the boy's hand in hers. Surprised by its unusual warmth, Dasia discovered a unique serenity in that tender moment that left her unexpectedly at peace.

Yet as she stared into Tannus's eyes, she simply could not find the strength to share any secrets of her own. For far too long had she been warned of what might happen if anyone discovered the truth about her family or her past, and the very last thing she wanted to do was risk whatever small chance of returning home she still had left.

"Here you go," Etta announced before entering the room once more, this time with four steaming glasses. "A little more tea ought to cheer us all up."

"Who's the extra glass for?" asked Dasia.

Smiling gently in response, Etta glanced at the picture of Ambra across the room. "I always make sure to save one for her, just in case she ever comes back home."

Dasia knew precisely how the old woman felt. And so desperate was she to see her beloved brother Demitris again that Dasia was convinced she could actually see him staring in at her from the snow-filled forest outside.

"Guessin' you're not thirsty," Etta said, her own glass of tea emptied just as swiftly as the one held by Tannus.

"Nah, I think I'm okay," Dasia said before setting her tea down.

"Well, can't say I blame you. These things have really got quite a kick. Now, why don't you two go on and grab your cloaks while I pack up some food? The Asterguards should be here soon, assumin' they can make it through all that snow without gettin' stuck."

Dasia turned her attention back outside once Etta returned to the kitchen, though by then, the apparition of Demitris was long gone.

"You sure you wanna do this?" Tannus asked quietly.

"What do you mean?" Dasia replied.

"Go back home, or wherever it is the Principal Preceptor wants to send you."

"It's not like I really have much of a choice," said Dasia. But as she watched Tannus stare out through the very same window, she could not help but wonder what sorts of strange ideas were tumbling around inside his mind.

"We could always just run away," he said suddenly. "Find a new home in the Ildarwood. Never have to worry about your mom and dad or my old gram ever again."

"But aren't these woods really dangerous? I mean, isn't that why no one's allowed to come out here till they're twelve?"

Tannus turned his attention back toward Dasia, his gaze unwavering. "When I was little, my mom used to read me all sorts of cool stories about the Ildarwood and all the unbelievable things that can happen out here. But my favorite one was about a brother and sister who were only eight years old when they were forced to run away after their whole village was attacked by monsters. My mom said the two kids were all by themselves when they made it into the woods, but then the forest helped them find a place to sleep and plenty of food to eat till someone finally came along who could keep 'em safe. She said the Ildarwood will always try to protect any kids in dire need, especially if they really don't have anywhere else to go."

But Dasia remained unconvinced. "Um, weren't you there last night when the Ildarwood actually tried to kill us?"

"Okay, sure. One lousy spirit tried to kill us. But right before that, a completely different spirit made sure I found you. And right after that, Etta came and found us. So maybe this all happened for a reason. Like, maybe me and you were supposed to meet out here and run away. That way, I don't have to live with my gram anymore, and you don't have to get ignored all the time by your mean old mom and dad. I mean, wouldn't that be amazin'?"

Dasia managed a gentle smile. "But won't we both get in a whole lot of trouble?"

Tannus smirked as he approached the front door and removed their cloaks from a rusty nail. "They'll have to catch us first."

III

The Night of Fateful Fires

W INDSWEPT SNOW WHIPPED Tannus's face as he ran through the forest that morning with Dasia following close behind. He had always hated the biting cold of winter, though never had he found it quite as soul-numbing as he had since first setting foot within the Ildarwood.

Longing for the warm hat and clothes his gram had spent weeks knitting, he could hardly believe how ungrateful he had been upon receiving them the night before. *I guess Gram was right again*, he lamented, though even that small concession felt like a frigid dagger to his pride.

"Won't the Asterguards just be able to follow our tracks?" Dasia asked as they climbed a steep, wooded hill.

"Not in this weather," Tannus breathlessly replied. Pausing to rest, he pointed back into the lower forest. "At this rate, they won't have any clear footsteps to follow, especially if we keep runnin' through spots where the snow's not as deep."

"It almost sounds like you've done this before."

"I used to play a game called 'howlin' hunters' with a bunch of friends when I was little," said Tannus, his mind racing back to those far happier times. "It was a lot more fun in the summer, when there were plenty of places to hide, but as soon as it started gettin' cold out, I always tried to stay inside. But then my dad would just tell me to toughen up and go outside, so I never really had much of a choice."

Resuming his slow march through the snow, Tannus could recall those days back in Silvermarsh like they had only happened the week before. "It was always a lot easier to be the hunter than the hider right after it snowed," he told Dasia. "That's when there weren't any other fresh tracks. But when it was still snowin' and windy like this, hidin' got a whole lot easier. At least, it did for me."

"I never got to play games like that when I was little," said Dasia, both arms wrapped tightly around herself for warmth.

"Why? Didn't you have any friends?"

"I had my older brother, Demy, but our mom and dad didn't like most of the other families in Marshwood, so they always told us to stay away from any other kids."

Tannus stopped and stared back at Dasia. "That sounds really lonely."

"It was," Dasia confessed.

Tannus turned his attention back toward the forest ahead and searched the horizon for any signs of shelter. Yet in the back of his mind, he could not stop thinking about how he had always felt so alone without any siblings to call his own. Someone to share in his memories and his struggles. Someone he had begun to think he might never have, especially after the night he had lost his closest friend.

Spotting the pale face of Fynn in the distance, Tannus wondered if the child he saw was in fact all that remained of the boy who had died back in Silvermarsh, or if it was merely some deception, either by a cruel and malicious spirit or perhaps just his own sad and lonely mind.

"Let's try goin' this way," Tannus suggested, motioning with his head in that direction.

For nearly an hour, Tannus and Dasia trudged together through feet of snow, with certain drifts even reaching as high as their chests. And even in those most agonizing moments, when others their age might have finally conceded defeat, the two weary travelers forced themselves to continue marching ahead, foot by arduous foot. Yet only once they had pushed through a wall of nearly impenetrable brush did they finally find some shelter.

Teetering on the edge of an embankment, which had been washed away by untold years of heavy rains, the crooked cottage had no doubt been a warm and welcoming place in its earlier days. Although time and the elements had taken a savage toll after decades of neglect, leaving it dangerously close to a sudden collapse.

"Looks good enough to me," Dasia said with a sigh of relief.

But before she could take even a single step closer, Tannus grabbed her by the arm. Recalling the terrifying story he had been shown by Nenika Osei mere weeks before, he stood paralyzed with fear at the prospect of inadvertently leading Dasia into a trap.

"Just wait here," he instructed. "I wanna make sure it's safe."

Sneaking inside with utmost caution, Tannus was surprised to find no signs of recent residents at all—not even any darkstride possums or nightmask raccoons. A short, decaying Ildarwood tree stood shimmering all alone in the center of the narrow entrance hall, its crystalline black bark crumbling into spectral dust beside its desperately wandering roots.

And aside from the uneven, splintered floors, which creaked time and again beneath his meager weight, there was a strange stillness in the air that left the home unusually quiet, even as storm-born gusts still raged in the forest outside.

"I think it's safe," Tannus called out to Dasia, who was all too eager to hurry in.

Taking a moment to look around, Dasia carefully ran her fingers along the countless messages carved into each wall by Ildarbound travelers long gone. "Looks like we're not the only ones who managed to find this place."

"Yeah, I think you're right," Tannus replied, his own attention focused solely on an overflowing basket, which had been conveniently left atop a battered old table in the center of a dust-covered kitchen. Overflowing with jars of water, food, and miscellaneous supplies, the basket had been carefully nestled between two fleece blankets, which had themselves been thoughtfully covered by a white linen sheet. "Whoever brought this here left a note," said Tannus, holding a small, unopened envelope out toward Dasia.

Taking care not to tear the paper as she opened it, she walked toward the nearest window to make better use of the room's only source of natural light. "'This place gave me shelter when I needed it most. Now I hope these supplies will help whoever finds it next. Best of luck, Deserei Nikamba.'" Dasia glanced at Tannus, moved by the incredible kindness of the mysterious girl. "You think we'll ever get the chance to thank her?"

"Thank her?" Tannus asked after spotting a small jar filled to the brim with chocolate treats. "I might have to hug her!" For far too long, he had been forced to satisfy his insatiable sweet tooth with his gram's ancient preserves and an assortment of severely bruised fruit from the market in town.

Proceeding into the home's stark living room, Tannus and Dasia glanced into the fireplace and discovered a heaping pile of sparkling ashes.

"Any chance you know how to light a fire?" asked Dasia, leaving Tannus half amused and half ashamed.

"I'm sure I can figure it out," he said with a sigh.

Nearly a dozen Ildarwood logs with iridescent bark had been stacked neatly beside the hearth, no doubt left behind by the same kind soul who had placed the basket in the kitchen. Tannus inspected each one carefully, just as his father had taught him. Nearly weightless yet somehow still heavy, each log seemed to retain enough dormant spectral energy to hold a steady Goldenfire flame.

Tannus needed only a minute to restack them all above the glimmering remnants of fires long extinguished. Yet by the time he had finished, he could not help but lament the house-like shape that lingered before him.

Standing once more, he found upon the mantel a single jar made of crystal-clear Ildarglass. Trapped within were three narrow twigs with ember-like veins, which gave off a warm golden glow.

"Those look like Candlewood," said Dasia, who had begun laying out a blanket on the bare living room floor. "My mom and dad use sticks just like those to light our fires and stoves."

"We had 'em in our house too," said Tannus. And the longer he stared at the jar's glowing contents, the more he found himself reminded of the radiant Candlewood tree that used to grow in the very center of his childhood home.

Removing a single stick from the jar, Tannus savored the ambient warmth that ran directly from his fingers into his heat-starved soul. All he needed to do was point the crystalline remnant and will it to ignite for it to release a powerful surge of the dormant power trapped within. An instant later, the carefully arranged stack burst into roaring spectral flames, sending radiant energy flowing swiftly throughout the house.

"Wow! I've never seen a fire do *that* before," said Dasia. "What's your secret?"

"Lots of practice," Tannus shamefully replied.

HOURS PASSED IN relative silence as Tannus and Dasia sat together by the fire, both bathing in the ambient heat that flowed like a fountain of pure energy directly into their severely weakened souls.

Little of substance did they discuss that afternoon, save for a few small stories here and there. Yet the longer they remained in each other's company, the more uncomfortable Tannus grew with each lingering stare of curiosity that Dasia cast in his direction.

"Once the snow stops, we'll need to find more food," he said to create a brief distraction. "My gram said there are a few farms with greenhouses out here, and it sounded like they can still grow food even in winter, so we should probably try to find one of those."

"You mean, like stealin'?" Dasia asked with a sour expression. "My mom and dad always said people lose a little bit of their soul every time they steal."

Stunned by her response, Tannus looked away just long enough to roll his eyes. "Well, then I guess we'll have to figure out a way to earn some Starlings. My gram said there are a bunch of places out here that'll pay Ildarbound for help. Maybe we can convince one of 'em we're just out here for our Trials."

"Yeah, that might work," Dasia said with a smile, even though she had serious doubts. "Look on the bright side: we'll never have to save money for firewood, because … well …" Then she gestured at the surrounding forest.

Managing a momentary smile himself, Tannus could hardly remember the last time he had actually enjoyed having a conversation, let alone with someone else around his age. "Does that mean you actually know how to chop wood?"

"Um, no. Not really," Dasia reluctantly confessed. "But I used to watch Demy do it all the time, so I'm pretty sure I could figure it out."

Tannus laughed at the very thought of someone as frail as Dasia trying to chop down and split an entire Ildarwood tree all by herself. And though she briefly shared in his amusement, her joy swiftly turned to sorrow, sending a sudden chill throughout the room.

"You really miss your brother, don't you?" asked Tannus.

"Yeah," Dasia replied with a sigh.

"Is that who the Mimicus was pretendin' to be when you saw it?"

"Yep," Dasia answered, her heart still broken over the ruse. "I can't believe I actually fell for it. I should've known the real Demy never would've forgiven me for what I did."

Silence returned to the crooked cottage as Tannus wrestled with an ever-growing sense of curiosity. "Would it maybe make you feel better if we talked about it?" he asked finally, a deep sincerity in his suddenly soft and humble voice.

"I don't know. I've never really told anyone what happened that night. My mom and dad said they'd never forgive me if I did."

"What if I told you what happened to me first? Would that help?"

Surprised by the offer, Dasia stared across the room at Tannus and carefully studied the subtle twinkle in his eyes. Within she could see a gentle sincerity she had only ever seen before in the eyes of Demitris himself.

"It might," she said finally, placing the burden on Tannus to trust her with his secrets first.

"Okay, so … I guess for me, everythin' started about two years ago, back when I was still livin' with my mom and dad in Silvermarsh …"

Staring deep into the vibrant spectral flames before him, he began to relive the very scenes he dared describe.

My mom's name was Elisa. I always thought she was the nicest lady in the world. She was one of those moms who love bakin' things for all the neighbors, and whenever she wasn't cookin', she was visitin' sick people all over town to help nurse 'em back to health. She said it was the least she could do to help the city recover, especially after all the riots.

My dad's name was Treyton, though everyone just called him Trey for short. He was probably the best woodcrafter in the whole city. At least, that's what my mom always said. I used to spend all my free time after school and on Restingdays watchin' him in his workshop. He always made the most incredible things out of Ildarwood, and people used to pay a ton of Starlings for 'em too.

They both treated me like gold, probably 'cause I was their only kid.

But whenever I wasn't in school or tryin' to learn as much as I could from my dad, they'd always make me play outside, especially whenever any of their friends came over to visit. They said it was important for me to try and make some friends of my own, but the only other kid I got along with was a really pale Aerish boy who said his name was Fynn.

We met when I was playin' a game of howlin' hunters, right after it snowed one day. I was tryin' to hide from some older kids when I noticed some fresh tracks in the snow. I just remember thinkin' how weird it was to see any footprints all the way out in those woods, 'cause my mom and dad always said no one even lived out there. So I decided to follow the tracks till I finally figured out whose they were.

The weird thing is, I almost didn't even see him hidin' at first. He was dressed in all-white clothes, and his skin and hair were just as white. But the weirdest thing about him was that his eyes were bright white too ... not like someone who's Broken, though. His were just different. I can still remember how much they sparkled and glowed, even in the middle of the day. They almost didn't seem real.

He was so scared to see me that I almost swore he was gonna wet his pants. But then I talked to him for a little bit, and after a while, he finally started talkin' to me. And I guess that's when we first started to be friends.

I spent over a year goin' to visit him at least once a week after that, whenever my mom and dad had people over and didn't want me hangin' around. And even though he didn't tell me very much about his family, he said he lived with his mom and dad, two brothers, and a little sister too. But he never told me any of their names or where exactly their house was ... only that he wasn't allowed to talk to anyone, or else he'd get in trouble.

So for a whole year, I never even mentioned him to my mom and dad. I just told 'em I was out with friends whenever I left the house, and as long as I never caused any trouble or got home too late, they were always happy.

But then one week in the middle of the fall, I went out to meet Fynn, and he never showed up. So I just figured he was sick or somethin', and went home. Then I went out to meet him again a week later, and still no Fynn. That's when I really started to get worried. But instead of just goin' home again … well, I guess I figured I should probably go check on him. So I did.

It took me a while to figure out where he lived, but I was able to get some idea by followin' the path he'd made through the woods whenever he came to see me. That eventually led me out to a small cabin that was so deep in the woods, there weren't even any roads.

Then came the tough part. I had to figure out how to sneak in through the spectral shield around their house without gettin' caught. The very last thing I wanted to do was get Fynn in trouble by showin' up uninvited. So I just stared at their Ildarstar for a few minutes and kept whisperin', "I'm just here to check on Fynn. Please don't sound an alarm." I couldn't believe it actually worked.

After that, I was able to sneak all the way over to the back side of his house. And when I peeked in one of his windows, well … that's when I saw him, tucked into bed with a wet cloth on his forehead and his mom doin' everythin' she could to help him get better. And he just looked so sick that I thought he might actually die, right then and there.

But what was really weird about the whole thing was that no one else in his family had the same white hair and skin as he did. They all just looked like normal Aerish people, with red hair and freckles, although his mom and dad both had Fynn's bright white eyes … especially after they prayed beside his bed.

I just remember feelin' so sad and helpless when I saw him. They all looked so scared … like they were desperate for a miracle to come and save him. And that's when it hit me. My mom helped save sick people all the time, so maybe she could figure out some way to help him too.

I ran all the way back home after that, and as soon as I caught my breath, I pulled my mom away from all her friends so I could tell her all about Fynn. I can still remember the scared look on her face when I was done. I honestly thought she was just as worried about him as I was.

I can still remember beggin' her to let me go with her before she left, but she said it just wasn't safe. I thought she was just afraid I might get sick too, or that Fynn's mom and dad would get really mad if we both just showed up outside their house. So then I just went up to my room, like she asked. And as soon as I closed the door behind me, I heard it lock all on its own.

I should've known somethin' was wrong as soon as that happened, but I just kept tellin' myself that my mom always went out of her way to help people in need. So I just sat on my bed and waited till I heard her leave the house.

But when I looked outside, it was the strangest thing. All of my mom and dad's friends just walked right past their carriages and out into the woods. And every single one of 'em was carryin' a Goldenfire torch and wearin' a hooded black cloak. And I guess that's when I knew for sure that somethin' was really, really wrong.

The problem was, I had no idea how to get out of my room. My mom and dad had told the house to lock me in, so I couldn't just open the windows or unlock the door. All I could do was beg the house to let me out. And I just remember gettin' madder and madder till I felt this weird burst of fire. Then the next thing I knew, half the door had exploded and knocked me right on my butt!

After that, I just ran downstairs as fast as I could and, well ... that's when I saw it. My mom and dad and all their friends had broken almost all the branches off the Candlewood tree in the middle of our house. I just couldn't believe it. It had always looked so strong, but that night, it just looked like it was all sad and defeated. And I guess I just felt so bad for it that I actually started cryin'.

The tree must've understood how I felt or somethin', 'cause right after that, it just opened the front door and let me out.

It didn't take me very long to find all the people with torches after that, but by the time I did, they had already made a huge circle around Fynn's cabin, just outside the invisible shield.

"Cillian Reid, we know you're in there," one man shouted. "Send the boy out to us, and nobody else has to get hurt."

Then the front door opened, and Fynn's father came out onto the front porch with an Ildarwood huntin' bow. "I don't know what you're all doin' here," he told 'em, "but if yas don't leave now, you'll be the only ones gettin' hurt."

"Quit wastin' our time!" the cloaked man hollered. "We know you've got an Astyrian boy hidin' in there, so just give him to us, and we'll go."

"He's not Astyrian!" Fynn's dad yelled back. "He's just got a condition that makes him look like one, I swear."

Well, all the people in cloaks weren't convinced. And after arguin' back and forth a few more times, they finally lost their patience. Then they all took off their cloaks, and every single one of 'em was wearin' golden Ildarglass armor. Some even had an Ildarglass mask over their nose and mouth ... probably so no one would ever know who they really were. But the scariest thing of all was the way their eyes glowed like little burning suns in the middle of the night. I'd never seen anythin' like it.

They started their attack by throwin' Goldenfire against the shield around the house. Then the Ildarstar start spinnin' really fast, and the warnin' noise it made was the loudest thing I've ever heard in my life. But they all just kept throwin' fire, and the star just kept gettin' smaller and smaller, so all the attackers just kept gettin' closer.

I remember the shield was almost about to fall when I started to see a whole bunch of stars in the sky start movin' all on their own. Then they all just streaked across the sky like bright, white arrows before finally fallin' and hittin' a whole bunch of the people around the cabin. It was incredible! But whatever those things were, they just weren't strong enough to stop all the angry people.

That was when Fynn's mom came outside to help his dad. Then there was a blindin' flash of light, and as soon as I looked back again, they were both wearin' Ildarglass armor too—only theirs was bright white. Then they started shootin' Ildarglass arrows at as many people as they could hit, but somehow even that wasn't enough to stop the attack.

The shield around the house fell a few minutes later. Then everyone on both sides pulled out an Ildarglass sword ... even my mom and dad. I just couldn't believe it. But Fynn's mom and dad just kept fightin'. And for a few minutes there, I thought they might actually win.

But then I saw my dad pull as much Goldenfire as he could out of some of the torches on the ground, and that's when I knew Fynn and his whole family were in trouble. I can still remember feelin' like my heart was about to stop when I saw my dad throw a giant fireball directly into the house. There was nothin' Fynn's mom and dad could do to stop it.

The whole cabin burst into flames after that, and I can still hear Fynn's parents screamin' for their kids before runnin' inside. But the entire time they were in there, all those horrible people outside just kept laughin' and cheerin' like it was the greatest thing they'd ever seen ... includin' my mom and dad.

Thankfully, Fynn's parents were able to save his brothers and little sister before the fire got too hot, but by the time they both tried to go back in for him, it was ragin' out of control. And no matter how much they prayed for protection, it just didn't seem to help. So everyone just stood outside and watched while the house burned down with Fynn inside.

Even after all this time, I'm still not sure what was worse ... watchin' everythin' that was happenin' to that poor family and knowin' it was all my fault, or hidin' in the woods like a scared little baby and feelin' like there wasn't anythin' I could even do to stop it.

I still don't know what made me decide to try and save Fynn after that. Maybe it was seein' my mom and dad lookin' so proud at what they'd done, or maybe it was seein' Fynn's mom and dad fallin' apart with their three other kids all cryin' beside 'em. But at some point that night, I just started runnin.' Past all the people in golden armor. Right past my mom and dad.

And straight past Fynn's whole family too. Then I just jumped inside, right through the spectral fire. I didn't even care that I kept gettin' burned, or that I was barely able to move from all the pain. I just kept lookin' for Fynn till I opened some random closet and found him hidin' in the back.

I tried so hard to convince him to leave, but he was just too weak and too afraid. And, well ... since everythin' that happened that night was all my fault to begin with, I guess I just figured the only thing left I could possibly do was crawl right into the closet beside him. At least that way, he wouldn't have to die alone. I can still remember how much he was shakin' before the floor and walls caved in around us. But even right there at the end, I never stopped holdin' on to him as tight as I could.

All I can remember after that is wakin' up in a Silverward with a bunch of stunned Healers and my old gram starin' down at me ...

Tannus fell silent as he recalled the look on his gram's face that morning. He had never seen her quite so worried or so relieved, let alone all at once. Thinking back to that fateful morning, he began to imagine how incredibly worried she must have been at that very moment back at home.

"What happened to Fynn?" Dasia asked solemnly, fearful she already knew the answer.

Breaking free from his momentary trance, Tannus glanced over at her and said, "Oh, um ... he ended up Broken after the fire. Then none of the doctors or Healers in the city were able to wake him up. So between that and bein' so sick even before the fire, he just ... died."

Tannus held back tears as those bitter words crossed his lips for the very first time. He had never spoken them to anyone before—not even his gram. Yet so moved by the story was Dasia that her tears flowed freely, leaving a sparkling mist in the air between them.

Reaching over to Tannus, she grabbed his hand and said, "I'm really sorry about your friend. But what you did to try and save him ... that was really brave. And you can't blame yourself for what your mom and dad did. You thought they were good people, and when you told 'em about Fynn, you were only tryin' to help."

"Yeah. A lot of help I was," Tannus grumbled, his teary gaze returning to the fire once more.

SNOW CONTINUED TO fall well into the evening that fateful day, leaving Tannus and Dasia free to explore the house and savor the sweet serenity of a quiet night in the Ildarwood. For over a year, both had dreamed endlessly of escaping into the vast and mythic forest, where countless legends had been written and countless more lives had been changed.

Lingering before the hollowed-out remnants of the Ildarwood tree in the home's main hall, Tannus wondered how many Ildarbound had stood in that very spot over the years. And for a few brief moments, he was tempted to touch the tree's sparkling bark just to glimpse whatever memories it still possessed. But as his fingers lingered mere inches away from the crumbling surface, he recalled his father's warning. *Never, ever try to see memories from any Ildarwood unknown ... not unless you're willing to pay a truly terrible price.*

An exchange of Silver from one's soul was the price most often paid, or so Tannus had always been told. A fair trade in the eyes of the tree, but one that far too often came with a grim and unpredictable tax. To glimpse into the memories of an Ildarwood tree, one would not just share in all the greatest joys it had ever witnessed—one must also risk bathing in the thick and murky waters of all its greatest sorrows. And if there was one thing Treyton Ambers had been determined to teach his beloved son, it was that the scars of the past could far too easily be transformed into fresh wounds in the present.

"I was thinkin' about before," Tannus said later that night, "and you don't have to tell me what happened to you and your brother if you really don't want to."

Surprised by his unexpected change of heart, Dasia finished the snack she had retrieved from a nearby jar and stared across the room at Tannus. Though she had been dreading the moment when she would be forced to relive the worst night of her life, some small part of her was excited to share her burden with someone who might actually understand her sorrows.

But before she could even begin to respond, a sudden knock at the door caused her and Tannus both to leap into the air with alarm.

"Who's that?" Dasia whispered.

"How am I supposed to know?" Tannus anxiously replied.

"My name is Garson Leck," a man called out through the door. "I'm an Asterguard looking for two lost children from town, so I was hoping for just a quick moment of your time."

Tannus and Dasia stared desperately at each other.

"Just a minute!" Tannus called out before returning his attention to Dasia and lowering his voice to a gentle whisper. "Pack up as much as you can. Then go out through the back door and hide. I'll see if I can convince him to leave."

"Are you sure?"

"No, not really. But I can't think of anythin' else, so ..."

A flurry of activity followed as Dasia frantically gathered their things and attempted to stuff them all back into their basket. Then she hurried across the house with utmost urgency before slipping outside through the home's rickety back door.

Another three knocks from the Asterguard followed before Tannus finally breathed a sigh of relief and hastily opened the front door.

"Everything okay?" the man asked sternly, his eyes immediately searching the visible portions of the house for any signs of distress.

"What? Yeah. Why? Oh, right. Sorry for makin' you wait. I was just ... you know ... in the bathroom ..."

The Asterguard studied Tannus's nervous expression for several seconds. "Would it be all right if I came inside?" the man asked politely.

"Um, yeah ... sure, I guess. Why not?"

After taking a few steps into the front hall, the Asterguard swiftly surveyed his surroundings. "We're trying to find two kids from town—an eleven-year-old boy and a ten-year-old girl. Sounds like they ran away late last night and were last spotted out by Etta's. Any chance you've seen them?"

"Nope. Definitely not," Tannus answered, making sure to keep his hands and forearms completely covered. Thinking back to a lesson from his gram, he recalled that every child in the Ildarwood was required to wear special leatherlike bracers until their Trials were complete. And according to her, they were the Preceptors' only reliable means of ensuring no Ildarbound soul could survive outside the forest for very long.

"You just find this place?" the Asterguard asked before taking a few more steps inside.

"No. Why? What makes you say that?" Tannus asked with surprise.

"You haven't replaced the Ildarwood tree yet. And you didn't bother to light a new Ildarstar."

"Oh, yeah, that ... well, I just didn't want any Cynders to find us."

"Us?" the Asterguard asked suspiciously. "Is there somebody else staying here with you?"

Suddenly irate with himself over such a careless slip of the tongue, Tannus shook his head and said, "No. I mean, not yet. I have some friends who are lookin' for somewhere safe to stay over the winter, and I think this place just might be it."

"I see," said the Asterguard, who proceeded to take a few more steps into the house. "So no one else but you here tonight?"

Sensing that the question was almost certainly a trap, Tannus turned away and began walking back into the living room, where a crackling spectral fire still burned brightly in the night. "I mean, I had a girl stop by for a while, but it was almost past her bedtime, so she just decided to head back home."

"Oh, really?" the Asterguard asked with amusement, slowly following Tannus. "And what was her name, if I may ask?"

Desperate to think of a quick answer, Tannus blurted out the very first name that came to mind. "She-na. Sheena Vyce. You probably know her dad from town. I think he owns a shop that sells … you know, chickens or somethin' … Sound familiar?"

"Not in the slightest," the Asterguard replied, "but I think that answers most of my questions. I'll just need to check one more thing before I go, if it's not too much trouble."

"Sure. Go right ahead," Tannus insisted, turning toward the fire and holding out his hands to savor its warmth.

"Can you do me a quick favor and roll up your sleeves?"

The short-lived charade was finally up.

Tannus lowered his head in defeat and let out a brief sigh. "I'm really sorry about this," he said solemnly. Then he threw out his right hand toward the Asterguard, channeling a surge of spectral flames in through his left palm and out toward the man in Ildarglass armor. It was an attack so entirely unexpected that the Asterguard did not even have a chance to react before his cloak and sleeves were engulfed in Goldenfire flames.

"You little brat!" he cried out, one hand smacking at his burning clothes in a frantic attempt to extinguish the spectral fire. Yet no matter how hard he tried, the Asterguard simply could not conjure enough Frostwater from within his soul to counteract its savage fury.

Watching with astonishment, Tannus could barely believe his eyes. It was a scene so traumatically familiar that it brought all his most terrifying memories directly to the forefront of his mind.

"What'd you just do?" Dasia asked with alarm, drawn back into the house by all the commotion.

"I think I just bought us some time," Tannus answered before grabbing her by the arm and dragging her over to the front door. He only needed to open it for an instant to spot the Asterguard's loyal companion—a majestic wulf composed entirely of Ildarwood roots and tangled vines.

Tannus could not have slammed the door any faster, and in so doing, he stopped the terrifying creature midleap with a deafening thud.

"I think maybe we should try sneakin' out the back instead," he said in a panic.

"Um, you think?" Dasia anxiously replied.

Rushing past the cursing Asterguard and the small spectral inferno that had surrounded him, Tannus and Dasia leaped out through the open back door and landed safely in the pristine snow beyond. From there, they ran as fast as their legs could carry them, both fully aware that their time to escape was fleeting.

A burning rage inside Tannus kept him warm as he raced through the snow with Dasia that night. Never before had he experienced the strange sensation of radiating heat surrounding him so entirely that he could actually see shimmering specks of golden energy trailing behind him like the tail of some magnificent burning comet.

"I can't believe you actually threw Goldenfire at an Asterguard," Dasia said as they ran. "How did you even manage to do that?"

"I'm not really sure," said Tannus. "It just sorta happens sometimes when I'm mad."

"Wait, you mean you've actually done it before?"

"Once or twice," Tannus lied, desperate to avoid scaring away his new friend before he had a chance to properly explain.

It was time he would not be given, for within seconds, the tell-tale sound of a wulf's howling cry pierced the silence of the night. The majestic beast had been set loose!

Pushing through feet of snow and bursting through briars and brush, Tannus and Dasia ran until the Ildarwulf's piercing blue eyes appeared in the distance far behind.

"We have to find someplace to hide, quick!" Tannus shouted. "A house. A cave. Anythin'."

But before they could even catch a glimpse of any shelter, the Ildarwulf was upon them. Leaping into the air, it lunged at Dasia first, only for Tannus to push her out of the way. And the very instant the creature's glistening teeth made contact with Tannus's swiftly raised arm, the Ildarwulf exploded into a tangle of sapphire roots.

Desperate to break free, Tannus tried to channel every last drop of his rage into the frigid, binding tendrils, but all his efforts were in vain. For no matter how much Goldenfire he summoned from within his soul, the Ildarwulf had far more Frostwater flowing through it to counteract the fiery effects.

And in those most hopeless of moments, Tannus could not speak. He could only cry out in pain as the creature's tightening roots constricted around him, draining more of his strength with each passing second. Catching a brief glimpse of Dasia as he struggled to break free, he could see the terrified look upon her face.

His final wish that night was for someone to come along and save her, no matter the cost. It was a wish they would both all too soon come to regret.

❧ IV ❧

Remnants of the Lost

TERROR FROZE DASIA'S heart as she watched the Ildarwulf's roots ensnare Tannus, leaving her helpless to intervene. And the more Tannus cried out for help, the more Dasia found herself reliving her own worst nightmare.

Before her eyes, she saw her brother Demitris struggling to breathe, his arms desperately reaching toward her as icy water splashed in all directions. All she wanted to do was reach out and save him. Yet no matter how much she wished for it in the deepest depths of her despair, she knew his fate could never be changed—though perhaps the fate of Tannus still could.

Grabbing ahold of the writhing, frost-filled tendrils before her, Dasia struggled to endure their stinging cold as she pulled with all her might. But just as she feared, the Ildarwulf reacted instantly, entangling her arms and leaving her just as helpless to break free.

Dasia's breaths hastened as panic set in. She would all too soon be entirely ensnared by the creature, and she could only imagine what manner of punishment would await once its master came to find it.

Convinced that she would be forced to spend the rest of her life locked up like Dustane, she envisioned herself never again seeing the warm light of day.

Those few moments of terror felt like eons as Dasia succumbed to the soul-numbing effect of the creature's frigid tendrils. Yet much to her surprise, she found a certain soothing comfort as waves of Frostwater surged directly into her heart. Within seconds, all her fears and uncertainties were gone, and every last ounce of emotional pain from her years of suffering had vanished as well. In their place, there was nothing left behind except for a cold yet tranquil void.

Neither she nor Tannus was prepared when a blinding flash of golden light lit up the night, inexplicably freeing them both in a violent flurry of flailing roots. Falling backward into a pile of snow, Dasia watched with disbelief as the creature exploded in the midst of spectral sparks and emerald flames.

What just happened? she wondered, her eyes barely able to focus. *Did Tannus just do that?*

Her answer came quickly. The sudden snap of a distant branch drew her attention toward a cloaked figure in the woods, but amidst the thick brush of the forest, Dasia struggled to see them clearly until they finally dared to approach.

"You two get into some trouble with the Asterguards?" the girl asked with a grin, a hunter's bow made of sleek gray Ildarwood held firmly in one hand.

"Yeah, somethin' like that," Tannus managed, the agonizing immensity of his pain all too clear in his voice.

"Well, anyone who's tryin' to get away from *them* is a friend of mine, so why don't you two hurry up and come with me? My pack has a house not too far from here, and I'm sure you could both use a nice warm fire and somewhere safe to lie low for a little bit."

Finally catching her breath, Dasia stared up at the girl and took a moment to study her face. Her eyes, though worn and tired, reflected a subtle glimmer of light, giving Dasia genuine hope that the stranger could be trusted.

"What's your name?" Dasia asked as the girl helped her up.

"You can call me Quill. Now, why don't we all get movin' before those Asterguards show up and ruin our night?"

"I don't know about you, but they've already ruined mine," said Tannus, both hands holding his throbbing head.

Yet as Dasia recovered from the intoxicating effects of the Ildarwulf's Frostwater-filled tendrils, she could not help but lament that the pain-numbing properties of the pale blue substance had already begun to wear off.

A CIRCUITOUS ROUTE through the forest made for a long trip to Quill's hideout that night, leaving Dasia and Tannus both on the verge of collapse.

"Don't worry," Quill assured them. "We're almost there."

Emerging at last before a run-down cabin, which was surrounded on all sides by steep, wooded hills and thick brush, Dasia eagerly breathed a sigh of relief.

"I'm surprised your house doesn't have an Ildarstar," she confessed as they approached the front door, taking note of the empty Asterport on the roof. "Isn't that dangerous?"

"Not as dangerous as havin' a giant glowin' beacon floatin' over you when you're tryin' to stay hidden," Quill replied. "Besides, Ildarstar hearts are expensive. And as soon as you go and ignite one, it's pretty much bound to that spot, so we can't just take it with us when we go."

"Sounds like you and your friends are on the move a lot," said Tannus.

"You would be too if you had any idea how dangerous these woods really are." Then Quill surveyed the surrounding forest one last time before finally leading her guests inside.

"Who're they?" a boy called out from his seat by the fire. Around the room, a dozen older Ildarbound kids in ragged clothes all turned their heads to stare at the two weary travelers.

"This one's Dasia, and he's Tannus," Quill answered. "I found 'em out near Dobb's Creek. The Asterguards sent an Ildarwulf after them, and they were pretty much goners till I showed up."

"You shouldn't have brought 'em here," the boy insisted, his eyes glowing emerald green for a moment. "The last thing we need right now is a bunch of Asterguards showin' up."

"They're not Ildarbound," Quill replied, catching Dasia and Tannus both by surprise. "It looks like they're both runaways, just like most of us were."

The boy remained silent as he considered Quill's words. Then a begrudging "Fine" soon followed. "But they can only stay one night. You'll have to take 'em somewhere else first thing in the mornin'. We've got enough mouths and souls to feed without addin' two more."

"We really appreciate it," Dasia offered, her gentle smile doing little to soften the boy's bitter expression.

"Don't mind Reinn," Quill whispered as she helped Dasia out of her cloak. "He doesn't trust anyone, and he's pretty much always in a bad mood."

"How'd you know we weren't Ildarbound?" Tannus asked abruptly, 'reluctant to remove his own cloak just yet.

"Well, for one thing, neither of you is wearin' a pair of bracers, so you obviously aren't twelve yet," Quill said with a laugh. "And for another, Asterguards never come out here unless they're lookin' for runaways or havin' problems with one of the adults. So if you two *were* Ildarbound, they'd have sent Preceptors or Ildarguards after you instead."

"I'm sorry, but … what are Ildarguards?" asked Dasia, earning a number of scoffs from Quill's friends.

"They're older kids who help the Preceptors patrol the woods and keep everyone safe," said Tannus. "My mom and dad were both Ildar-guards durin' their Trials, so they always wanted me to be one too."

"Don't waste your time," said Quill. "The Ildarguards out here are pretty much useless. They never show up when you actually need 'em, and whenever they do show up, they only ever make things worse. Now, why don't you two just go find a spot in there and make yourselves at home? I've gotta head back out, since it's still my night to patrol. Oh, and try to stay away from Reinn. He can be a bit … *weird* with new people. And people he knows, actually. So really, everyone."

"Weird how?" Dasia asked nervously.

"Just try not to bother him, and hopefully, you won't have to find out."

Dasia glanced at Tannus, but his attention was focused solely on the strange boy with emerald-green eyes staring back at him.

"So you two are runaways too, huh?" one girl asked as they approached. With long black hair and matching eyes, she had a crooked smile that made her rosy cheeks even more prominent against the back-drop of her pale complexion. "My name's Raeven. And that's Sage, Thrash, Frostie, Wade, Jett, and Scorch. There are a few others you'll meet in the mornin', but they're either in bed already or out on patrol."

"I really like your name," said Dasia. "Actually, I've never heard of any of your names before … at least, not as names."

"That's 'cause we all got new names after we first came out here. Some 'cause we chose 'em, and others 'cause they were earned."

"Wait, you mean you're actually allowed to do that?" Dasia asked with surprise.

"Yeah, of course," Raeven answered. "As soon as our Trials start, we can change our names, our looks … sometimes even our lives, if we're lucky. Those are some of the oldest laws of the Trials. Of course, most kids out here don't even bother to change their names, but for those of us who do, the names we choose usually fit a whole lot better than the ones we were given. Plus, the Trials are supposed to be our one real chance to start our lives over, so havin' new names really helps with that. And in a weird way, it kinda helps you feel like all the awful stuff you had to live through growin' up never really happened, so it's a whole lot easier to try and leave it all behind."

"I love that," said Dasia, one hand placed gently over her heart.

"Is gettin' one of *those* part of your Trials too?" Tannus asked abruptly, far more interested in Raeven's Ildarglass sword than anything else.

Raeven smirked as she drew the weapon from its sheath. "What, this?" she asked while proudly brandishing the long, jagged blade. "Nah, we have to make these ourselves. Normally, a sword like this would have a Silverwood handle, since those make the cleanest blades, but out here, you've just gotta make do with whatever you can get, so all of our weapons are made with Spitewood instead. It's pretty hard to find out here, and the blades aren't all that great, but it's a whole lot better than nothin'."

"Wait, you mean you actually have to use *swords* to survive out here?" Dasia asked as a tight knot formed in the pit of her stomach. She had never been particularly fond of any form of fighting.

"Swords. Bows and Ildarglass arrows. Throwin' stones. Whatever it takes," said Raeven. "Not everyone out here is able to control a spectral element well enough to protect themselves in a fight, so these help us even the odds."

"Does that mean there really *are* monsters in the Ildarwood?" Dasia asked next, her gaze instinctively finding Tannus for support.

Raeven laughed and shrugged as some of the older kids chuckled. "The Ildarwood is full of dangerous things. Monsters. Trees. Plants. Animals."

"Cynders," Tannus interjected, drawing the full attention of everyone nearby.

"Yeah. Some of those too," said Raeven.

"Um, what are Cynders?" Dasia dared to inquire, keenly aware of the sudden shift of emotions throughout the room.

"I learned about 'em from the Overseer in Silvermarsh," said Tannus. "She said Cynders are ruthless creatures created by the Trials. Failing Ildarbound with corrupted hearts who only ever want one thing—to hunt innocent kids and steal as much Silver from their souls as they can get."

"That's awful," Dasia replied, utterly stunned that other children could ever be so cruel.

"Worse than you could ever imagine," said Raeven. "But I'm surprised you've heard of 'em. Most kids outside the Ildarwood don't even know what the word 'Cynders' means. They're supposed to be a surprise for new Ildarbound. The scary, faceless hunters that always attack on First Day. That way, all those poor, helpless kids will take their Trials seriously from that point on."

"Have you ever met any?" asked Dasia. "Cynders, I mean."

"A few. Though some are worse than others. Most are just tryin' to figure out how to stay alive out here, but some of 'em really enjoy hurtin' others. It's almost like they're actually addicted to makin' people suffer. Those are the ones you've really gotta look out for. Like this one pack we met at the start of our first year, they always dipped all their arrows in venomic toxins from a vinevus, just to make sure anyone they hit kept on sufferin' … even after the wound was healed."

"Do I even want to know what a vinevus is?" Dasia whispered to Tannus.

"It's a really dangerous animal that looks just like a little tangle of briars," said Tannus, his eyes still focused on Reinn. "Their vines are covered in glowin' green thorns made of Ildarglass, and my dad said they use 'em to paralyze their prey. We were followed by one once in the woods behind our house. He had to throw a whole bunch of Goldenfire just to scare it away. And when I asked why he was so worried about it, he said their venom contains a really nasty kind of Stormspark that makes you relive all your worst memories and nightmares every minute of every day, sometimes for years."

Dasia fell silent for a moment as she tried to imagine such horror. "*That's* what some of the Cynders are usin' to hurt people? But ... why would anyone ever choose to be that mean?"

"'Cause some of the kids out here are just that desperate to survive," said Raeven, a heavy sadness in her voice. "The deeper into the Ildarwood you go, the more dangerous things get, and the harder pure Silver is to find. That's why some kids will do whatever it takes just to keep their souls alive."

"I'd never want to hurt someone else," Tannus said firmly. Only then did he finally draw the full and undivided attention of Reinn.

"Come on, now, Tannus," he said sternly. "You don't need to lie to any of us."

"I'm not lyin'," Tannus insisted. "Only monsters hurt innocent people for fun."

"Yeah, except that wasn't what you said. You said you'd never want to hurt someone else. But that's not true, is it? You actually *enjoy* hurtin' other people, if you think they deserve it. Now, isn't that right?"

Tannus opened his mouth to speak but found no words.

"Watch this," Raeven whispered to Dasia. "Reinn can always tell when someone's lyin'. He can sense people's intentions just by lookin' in their eyes. And sometimes, if he really looks hard enough, he can even see their memories."

"It felt good, didn't it?" Reinn asked suddenly. "When you tried to punish all those people who hurt you. You probably savored the thought of their sufferin'. I'll bet you even tried to call it justice."

Dasia stared at Tannus with utter disbelief over what she was hearing, but no matter how hard Tannus tried, he simply could not stop staring into Reinn's intense emerald eyes.

"What's he talkin' about, Tannus?" asked Dasia, who found herself increasingly afraid of her companion.

"Go ahead and tell your little friend the truth," said Reinn, who finally rose from his seat to walk toward Tannus. "Tell her how good it felt to turn all that pent-up rage into punishment for the people you hated so much. Tell her how excited you got each and every time you did it. It was almost like an addiction, wasn't it? An addiction you were powerless to resist. An addiction you still crave, even now as you're starin' up at me. In fact, I'll bet you'd like nothin' more than to punish me for whatever terrible things you think I've done. Now, isn't that true?"

Tannus stood, trembling but resolute, his burning gaze locked upon Reinn—neither one willing to flinch.

"I know what you are," said Tannus, earning a grin from Reinn and several of the other boys seated around him.

Only then did Dasia notice the subtle changes to almost every face around the room. One by one, they began to disappear behind a truly terrifying spectral mirage, leaving nearly all of them looking more like monsters than teenage kids.

"Then say it," Reinn commanded, his teeth glistening in the flickering light of the nearby fire. "What are we?"

Dasia gasped as the terrible realization hit her at last. "Cynders."

The next thing she knew, Tannus had pushed Reinn away with one hand while simultaneously pulling a stream of Goldenfire from across the room with the other. Forcing it to flow directly through him, he channeled every ounce of the ferocious spectral flames back out toward the roomful of Cynders, sending all but Reinn ducking for cover.

Stunned silence followed as an emerald glow around the strange boy absorbed every sparkling fleck of energy from the attack, drawing it deep into his soul and causing his eyes to glow even brighter than before.

"My turn," Reinn said viciously. He took only an instant to savor the panicked expressions of Dasia and Tannus before swiftly thrusting one hand forward, releasing a blinding bolt of emerald lightning directly toward them.

Tannus tackled Dasia to the floor without a second thought, barely saving them both from the savage attack. A deafening explosion immediately followed, sending verdant flames and shards of Ildarwood from the nearest wall in all directions.

"Run!" Tannus shouted. Thinking only of Dasia, he frantically summoned wave after wave of spectral fire into his hands before hurling each one at a different attacker.

"Where do you think you're goin'?" one of the Cynders shouted, his feet firmly blocking Dasia's path as she scrambled toward the door.

Dasia froze, her eyes staring up at the boy's monstrous visage. Desperately wishing that she had any gifts like those of Tannus, she tried to imagine some practical way to attack the Cynder. But so overwhelmed with fear had she become that when she threw her hand forward, only the most minuscule little sparkle shot out into the air.

"Ha!" the Cynder crowed before being blasted by Tannus.

"What are you waitin' for? Go!" Tannus shouted.

Bright streaks of Goldenfire, Stormspark, and Frostwater soared over Dasia's head as she ran back out into the snow with Tannus. Neither one had ever run quite so fast.

"Let the hunt begin!" Reinn shouted from the cabin's front porch.

Within seconds, flashes of light lit up the night as Ildarglass arrows exploded time and again against the crystalline bark of nearby trees. Yet only a single arrow needed to hit its mark for Dasia to collapse into the snow with a deafening scream.

"What? What's wrong?" Tannus implored. "Were you hit?"

"It's my arm! It hurts so much!" Dasia cried out, one hand desperately grasping her upper arm. She had never before seen so much Silver. Flowing like a river of shimmering energy, it evaporated into a sparkling mist almost instantly, then drifted swiftly in the direction of the one ruthless Cynder who had let loose the fateful shaft.

"We need to find somewhere to hide, quick," said Tannus. Yet only after spotting a familiar glow in the distance did he dare lead Dasia toward the edge of a steep, wooded hill. "Hold on!" he shouted. "We're about to go for a really wild ride."

Dasia had no time to prepare before Tannus pulled her close and leaped into the darkness. Using his cloak like a makeshift sled to navigate between trees and bushes, he narrowly avoided certain disaster time and again, leaving Dasia breathless with panic. Only once they had reached the bottom in one piece did she finally dare exhale.

"What the heck is wrong with you?" she shouted. "We could've died!"

"I'm sorry," Tannus replied with no true sincerity. "Would you rather get roasted by Cynders? 'Cause we can always go back."

"I ... we ... argh! Now what are we supposed to do?"

Tannus glanced at the babbling brook nearby and considered their options. "They can't follow us through the snow if we don't leave tracks," he said, recalling another lesson from his father. "Come on. Let's go."

"What? No way!" said Dasia, her gaze focused solely on the brook's frozen banks. "Do you have any idea how cold that water's gonna be?"

"Again, frozen or roasted? Your choice. But I know which way I'm goin'."

Watching as Tannus waded into the brook and began sloshing his way upstream, Dasia shook her head with disbelief. "I'm gonna end up freezin' to death out here," she mumbled before following Tannus into the water and gasping at the sudden shock of its frigid sting. Momentarily transported back to the fateful night when her brother Demitris had tragically fallen into a frozen lake, she began to wonder if all her suffering in the Ildarwood was somehow her punishment for past crimes.

"I see light up ahead!" Tannus called back to her. "We're almost there."

It was not a moment too soon. Staring up at the sheer cliffs around her, Dasia marveled at all the glowing ice, which clung to every granite rock face wherever pristine streams of snowmelt cascaded down like endless tears. At their feet, half a dozen old mines had been dug deep under the Ildarwood, leaving piles of boulders and stone debris wherever Dasia looked.

"Tannus," she managed before suddenly collapsing into the brook, her immense exhaustion finally overwhelming her.

The last words she heard were his desperate cries into the night.

"Please! Can somebody come and help my friend?"

My friend.

"DASIA? HEY, CAN you hear me?"

It was the voice of a stranger, soft and soothing, that greeted her later that night. Slowly awakening as the sound and sparkle of a warm spectral fire nearby caught her attention, Dasia found herself staring up into the gentle face of a teenager with glowing white eyes.

"Who ... who are you?" Dasia managed, suddenly alarmed by the unexpected absence of Tannus.

"My name's Wren. And try not to worry. You're perfectly safe here, at least for now. Your friend's just keepin' an eye out for Cynders while I work on closin' your wound."

Dasia briefly surveyed the rough-hewn tunnel around her. Cold, damp, and uninviting, it was a far cry from the welcoming warmth of the crooked cottage. "Am I gonna be okay?" she asked nervously, her gaze finally returning to Wren.

"That arrow did a lot more damage than Tannus thought," Wren answered while tending to the glowing mark on Dasia's upper left arm. "By the time you got here, your soul had almost completely run out of Silver. Lucky for you, I've had more than a few run-ins with Cynders myself over the past year, so I knew exactly how to patch you up. See? Nothin' left but a little spectral scar."

"Thank you," Dasia timidly replied, her attention momentarily lingering on the cold white glow left behind by the wound. "It still hurts a little bit."

"It'll always hurt a little if you stop and think about it. My mom used to say that's just a soul's way of remindin' us not to do somethin' stupid enough to get hurt that way again. Just try not to think about it too much, or you'll end up makin' it bleed Silver all over again."

Managing a weak smile of gratitude for the stranger's kindness, Dasia took note of Wren's elaborate shirt and skirted pants—a distinctive style worn only by a privileged few in Selyrian society. "You're Anderen?" she said with surprise.

"Last time I checked," Wren cheerfully replied.

It had been over a year since Dasia had seen someone like Wren. With spirits that transcended the constraints of "man" and "woman," Anderens were renowned for possessing some of the best qualities of both, yet with unique perspectives and traits all their own.

"It's just … I thought all the Anderens born around here had to go to Mount Greiloch for their Trials."

"Most of us do. But why would I ever want to be just like everyone else?"

Amused by the notion, Dasia shrugged and said, "All I've ever wanted was to be like everyone else. I guess I just thought my life would be a whole lot easier that way."

"Nobody ever changed the world after havin' an easy life," Wren replied before finding a seat beside the fire.

"I've never wanted to change the world," said Dasia. "I just wanted to feel happy … and safe."

"Sometimes the only world we can change is our own. But isn't that still a cause worth fightin' for?"

Dasia blinked, entirely unprepared for such a sage response. "I don't know. I've never really been much of a fighter."

"Well, if you won't stand up for yourself, then who will?"

Dasia shrugged and looked away. For years, it had always been Demitris who had stood up for her. But ever since his death, Dasia had found it impossible to do or say anything on her own behalf. And perhaps worse, she could not even imagine standing up for herself or anyone else ever again.

"So, what brings you all the way out here?" Wren asked before throwing another Ildarwood log on the fire. "You're obviously not Ildar-bound."

Dasia swiftly lowered her sleeve to cover her bare forearm, even though the damage had already been done. "We both decided to run away from home," she answered timidly, ever fearful that Wren might turn on her too.

"Yeah, I already heard that whole story from Tannus. But what brings *you* out here? Somethin' tells me there's more to your story than anythin' he's said so far."

"I ... I'm not sure what you mean," said Dasia, desperate to avoid Wren's penetrating stare. Yet the longer they looked at her, the more convinced she became that Wren was somehow gazing beyond what any normal eyes could see.

"I can tell you're different," Wren said softly. "I'm just not sure how."

Dasia looked away before attempting to explain. "I was born a twin," she began, "but my brother Dustane ... well, he's gone. Not dead gone, just ... locked away so no one will ever see him again."

"No wonder your eyes look so empty," said Wren, whose expression had quickly become more somber. "The Preceptors say a person's eyes are the windows to their soul, and when I look into yours, I see so much loneliness and regret." But before Dasia could look away again, Wren gently touched her arm and said, "But I can also see a little light ... like maybe you're finally startin' to let yourself feel hopeful again."

Dasia managed a fleeting smile, forever timid beneath the imposing weight of anyone's full attention.

"It's okay. We don't need to talk about it if you don't want to," said Wren. "But you should at least talk to Tannus. He's really worried about you, and sometimes all anyone really needs to feel less lonely is someone who actually cares enough to listen. Someone we can trust who only wants to see us happy and keep us safe."

Dasia glanced at Wren, suddenly moved by their words, yet still too afraid to speak.

"Why don't I go get him? Maybe you two can have a nice talk before gettin' some rest."

"Okay," Dasia managed, her attention returning to the fire as Wren stood up and vanished into the darkness.

It took only a few minutes for Tannus to appear, his sparkling eyes reflecting the bright spectral flames near Dasia, even as his pallid expression betrayed the seemingly endless hours he had spent worrying.

"Feelin' better?" he asked before sitting down across from her.

"Yeah, a little bit," Dasia replied.

"Listen … I'm really sorry about what happened before. I knew somethin' was off about all those kids, but by the time I finally figured out what it was, it was just too late. I never, ever meant for you to end up gettin' hurt."

"It's not your fault," Dasia insisted. "They seemed so nice, and we had no way of knowin' what they really were. But …"

"But what?"

"Was it true what they said? The stuff about you kinda bein' just like one of *them*?"

Tannus scoffed at the very notion. "I'm not a Cynder. I'm nothin' like any of them. I swear."

"Then why did Reinn say all that stuff? And why did it bother you so much when he did?"

Tannus fell silent and looked away. "After everythin' that happened to me back in Silvermarsh, the Healers said I was lucky I hadn't ended up Broken, like Fynn. My gram said it was 'cause pretty much everyone in our family has Goldenfire runnin' through their veins, so that must've somehow kept me safe. But she also made sure to warn me that

I'd never be the same after that night. She said what happened was bound to change me. That all that Goldenfire and all those awful memories would make me angry all the time … and maybe even dangerous, if I wasn't careful. That's why I decided to go live with a foster family instead. I guess I just didn't wanna end up hurtin' her by mistake."

Dasia stared at Tannus intently from across the fire. "Then why do I feel like there's more you're not tellin' me?"

"My gram was right. I *was* dangerous, and I *was* angry. I couldn't stop thinkin' about how some of the people who went after Fynn that night barely even got in any trouble after. So every few weeks after everythin' happened, I ended up sneakin' out in the middle of the night and … well, I guess I just wanted to try and make sure they all got punished for what they did."

"Punished how?" asked Dasia, even as she feared learning the truth.

"By tryin' to do to them what they did to Fynn," Tannus reluctantly confessed.

A gasp from Dasia followed, but Tannus immediately shook his head and said, "It didn't work. No matter how many times I tried, I was never able to throw enough Goldenfire at most of the houses to do any real damage. But I wanted to so bad, and just knowin' how scared they all were after they realized what had happened … I don't know … I guess it just made me feel a whole lot better. Like all of a sudden, maybe they finally understood what real fear felt like. But the sad thing is, a part of me still wishes I had actually been able to hurt them more."

Silence followed as Dasia struggled to process everything that Tannus had confessed.

"I'll understand if you never wanna talk to me again," he said nervously, his gaze desperately avoiding her own.

"I still haven't told you about the night my brother died," Dasia replied, catching Tannus by surprise.

"Are you sure?" he asked, meeting her gaze.

Dasia nodded, even as she feared having to relive those terrible scenes all over again. "You're not the only one who wishes they could change the past," she said solemnly. Yet only after staring into the fire for several moments did she finally dare to tell her version of the truth about her past.

When I was born, my mother gave birth to me and my brother Dustane at the exact same time, and she said we were holdin' a single spectral stone. She said that made us special. Like, more than twins. Like we actually shared a soul. But accordin' to her, most twins like that don't survive for very long—so she was forced to choose which one would live … and which one would die.

She wanted to choose me over Dustane. The only problem was, if she made the wrong choice, and Dustane's half of the soul was actually stronger than mine, then, well … I would've been lost too. So my dad convinced her not to risk it, and they decided to bring us both home instead. But ever since that night, they always made sure to keep Dustane hidden away where no one could ever find him. That way, they could always be sure my part of the soul would stay alive.

After that, they probably didn't think about him all that much till I was old enough to talk. I guess that's when I surprised 'em both by startin' to ask all sorts of questions about Dustane. It was like I could somehow sense my other half was somewhere in the house, even though I'd never really seen him. So that was the first time they told me no one could ever find out about him or all the things they'd done to keep me safe. Otherwise, they'd never see either one of us ever again.

A few years later, they decided to move us all from Marshwood to Amberdale. And the night of their housewarmin' party, they invited a whole bunch of people over. That way, they could make friends with all the most important people in town. But after they sent me and my older brother, Demy, off to bed, I just remember hearin' a strange whisper in the middle of the night. It was like someone just kept sayin' my name. I still don't even know how I was able to hear it from all the way upstairs.

I snuck down to the first floor without anyone knowin', and that's when I heard my mom and dad talkin' to one of the really old men from the party. They wanted to know if it was safe to get rid of Dustane before I started my Trials, and they wanted to make sure no one would ever know he had ever existed at all.

I just couldn't believe they would actually do that to their son, and I must've made a noise, 'cause then they all went quiet. Then my mom said she was gonna go check on me, so I ran all the way back up to my room and locked the door behind me. I just didn't know what to do ... but I knew for sure that I didn't want Dustane to get hurt. So I walked over to the strange door in my room they were usin' to keep him locked away, and I somehow managed to unlock it.

When I opened the door, Dustane's room looked dark and empty, so I took just a few small steps inside. But then I saw his eyes. They were the coldest shade of blue I'd ever seen, and they were glowin' so bright they practically lit up the whole room. Then I just remember feelin' a gust of cold air, almost like he ran right through me.

I don't really remember what happened after that, but my mom and dad told me everythin' the next mornin'. They said Dustane had run outside, right past them and down the huge hill across the road. And I guess they just didn't think he'd listen to either one of them, so they sent Demy to go out and bring him back instead.

I'm still not sure if either one of 'em even realized where they were goin', but they both ended up runnin' across the lake at the bottom of the hill. It was mostly frozen from all the cold, but for some reason, one part in the center wasn't anywhere near as thick as all the rest. The first thing they heard was the cracks formin' in the ice. My mom said it sounded like two metal poles smashin' against each other. Demy didn't even try to run back to the shore. For some reason, he just stopped. Then the ice shattered right under his feet, and Demy just ... fell in.

Dustane ran back and tried to save him, but there was nothin' he could *do. The ice was just too thin. So he had to watch on helplessly while Demy died. None of that ever would've happened if I hadn't gone and let him out.*

My mom and dad didn't even have to Break poor Dustane after that. His part of our soul was pretty much gone. It was just so cold and small that I couldn't even sense it anymore. All they had to do was lock it away some-where safe. And as soon as they could finally find someone to buy the house, the three of us just packed up and moved to Ranewood. They said it was the only way they could leave everythin' they wanted to forget about behind. Well, everythin' but me.

Pale blue tears fell from Dasia's cheeks as she shook her head with deep regret. "They never forgave me for what happened," she told Tan-nus. "And I can't really blame 'em. I mean, I don't think I'll ever even be able to forgive myself."

A deafening silence followed as Dasia anxiously awaited a response. "Please say somethin'," she whispered.

Tannus stared across the fire at her. "You were tryin' to save his life, and you had no way of knowin' what'd happen after that. Besides, your mom and dad were the ones who said they'd risk your life to get rid of Dustane, so you can't really blame yourself for what happened. It just wasn't your fault."

"Well, if what happened to me wasn't my fault, then I guess that means what happened to you wasn't yours."

Tannus opened his mouth to speak, but no words dared emerge. All he could offer was a momentary smile, which was met ever so briefly by one from Dasia in turn. Both wanted so very desperately to believe those simple words. Neither truly could.

Guided by the Light

YOU'RE UP EARLY."

No one regretted it more than Tannus. After weeks of living with his gram, he could hardly believe that he would still awaken at dawn, even in the darkness of a seemingly endless tunnel beneath the Ildarwood.

"Any sign of Cynders?" he asked Wren, who had stayed up all night to watch the entrance.

"Nope. Though I can't really say I'm surprised. Even when they're mad, they don't usually like to hunt in the middle of the night. And I don't think I've ever seen 'em bother to leave their camps before mid-mornin'. Unlike you, they seem to enjoy sleepin' in."

Watching as the first hints of sunlight appeared over the treetops of the Ildarwood, Tannus allowed himself a few moments to soak in the serenity of the scene before him. He had never before seen a sunrise over the forest. More idyllic than anything he could have imagined, the golden horizon ever so slowly banished all lingering darkness from the night, leaving a bright blue sky to reign proudly in its place.

"Your little friend is worried about you," Wren warned him. "And I'm not talkin' about the one who's still sleepin' by the fire."

Confused at first, Tannus glimpsed back into the tunnel. Only then did he spot the ghostly figure watching from the shadows. "Wait ... you mean, you can see him too?"

"Not like you can," Wren said with a smile, "but I know he's there. His soul and mine are both blessed by Asterlight, so to me he looks more like a beacon than a boy, but I can still sense his emotions."

"You have any idea what he wants?"

"Isn't it obvious? He's been tryin' to protect you. And for some reason, he really wants to help you protect Dasia too."

"Any chance you can ask him why?"

"I'm not *that* gifted," Wren answered with amusement. "But one of the less pleasant Preceptors out here taught us that some spirits can actually sense what might happen in the future. And if they don't like what they see, they'll sometimes do as much as they can to stop those things from comin' true."

"Yeah, Etta warned us some ghosts could do that," Tannus confessed, earning another chuckle from Wren.

"Your friend's not a ghost. He's a spectre."

"Okay ... so, what's the difference?"

"Most ghosts are just hollow shells of their former selves, and they can't ever leave the place they haunt. All they can do is repeat the same old routines from their life over and over again till all their Silver is gone. But spectres are special. Their souls are still pretty much whole, and they're forever bound to a single object, person, or place that was really important to them while they were still fully alive. And accordin' to Ms. Rondles, they will never find rest in Ildaris, the World Beyond Our World, till whatever last mission they've given themselves is finally complete. So, if I had to guess, I'd say his must be to protect the two of you."

"But why would he even want to do that? Especially after everythin' that happened 'cause of me ..."

"Isn't it obvious?" Wren replied with a shrug. "He must not blame you. And if that's true, then I've really gotta ask ... why are you still blamin' yourself?"

Staring into Wren's bright white eyes, Tannus searched for the answer to that very question. "I guess it's just a whole lot easier than bein' mad at everyone else."

"You can't stay mad forever. Sooner or later, all that Goldenfire in your heart will eat a hole right through it. And once that happens, you'll end up just like every other angry person in the world who'd rather go out and hurt someone than figure out how to help 'em instead. Sound familiar?"

Tannus thought first of the Cynders he had met the previous night. But after another long moment of reflection, he recalled all the ruthless people who had attacked Fynn and his family the year before. Disgusted by the mere notion of one day turning into one of those cruel and heartless monsters, he shook his head with immense contempt. "I will *never* be like any of the people who hurt Fynn," Tannus insisted. "I just wish I knew why they even wanted to attack him in the first place. I mean, it doesn't make any sense. He was just a helpless little kid."

Wren sighed as they stared off into the sea of silver Ildarglass leaves outside. "In some parts of the world, people fear darkness. In this part of the world, people fear light. And around here especially, that's all because of the Astyrians. Their faith has them convinced that there will one day be a war, with all the souls aligned toward Asterlight on one side and literally everyone else on the other. So their only purpose in life is to convert as many people as possible while trying to eliminate all the rest. I guess, in their minds, that's the only way to make sure they'll have a stronger army whenever the War for Ildaris finally comes.

And I've heard that's why they decided to invade Selyria over fifty years ago.

"Now, I know most folks don't like talkin' about it, but a whole lot of kids our age have parents and grandparents who had to live through their reign. And I'm sure most of 'em saw things we can't even imagine. A few probably even had to do some pretty awful stuff just to survive. And yeah, the Astyrians eventually lost, and they were all forced to leave, but that doesn't mean most people will ever be ready to forgive 'em for what they did. Not after twenty years of brutal war.

"So if you put yourself in their shoes, it kinda makes sense that they'd never want anyone even remotely like the Astyrians to rise to power ever again. The only problem is, some folks hate the Astyrians so much, they don't even care that genuinely good people can have souls aligned toward Asterlight too. All they see is an enemy. Someone who needs to be stopped before they go and start another war."

"Do you ever have to deal with that kind of hate?" Tannus asked reluctantly. "I mean, 'cause of the color of your eyes."

"Sometimes," Wren answered. "And if I was like every other Anderen I know, I'd probably spend the rest of my Trials tryin' to align my soul back toward Silver. In fact, I'm sure that'd save me from all sorts of headaches down the road."

"So why won't you?" asked Tannus, desperate to understand their seemingly irrational decision.

Wren managed a gentle smile, then stared out toward the Ildarwood and said, "Well, if the Heavens never make mistakes, then I must've been born this way for a reason. I just need to figure out what that reason is."

"Any guesses?" Tannus asked with a smirk.

"Probably the same reason you found Dasia. The spirit world always strives for balance."

"I don't understand," said Tannus.

So Wren took a moment to recite a poem they had learned early on in their Trials:

Too much fire, all will burn.
Too much cold, then frost in turn.
Too much thunder, signals pain.
Too much water, tears will reign.
Too much wind, a threat unseen.
Too much stone, and faults to glean.
Too much light, then blinded sight.
Too much dark, then endless night.

Noting the quizzical expression on Tannus's face, Wren explained, "Right before the Astyrians invaded, Ildarwood forests all over the world became infected by an ancient corruption called the Blight. It was a contagion of the soul that could kill healthy Ildarwood trees in days and turn even the most friendly hearts feral in a night. And I guess it got so bad at one point that these woods and everyone in 'em were almost destroyed, so the Astyrians arrived to try and stop it. But after they went too far, thousands of souls aligned toward darkness needed to rise up and fight against 'em till a proper balance could be restored."

"So you think souls like yours and Fynn's will help prevent another Blight?"

"Exactly. There must always be balance in the Ildarwood. Light and darkness. Fire and ice. Your soul and hers."

"But she can't even control a spectral element yet. How can you be so sure it'll end up bein' Frostwater?"

"I can see it in her eyes. Her experiences in these woods, the people she's met ... her time with you. I think they're all helpin' her see that the world isn't really as cold and lonely as she always thought it was. But until she finally lets go of her past and figures out who she really is at heart, she'll never be able to master her true gifts. And without her gifts, I doubt she'll be able to survive out here for very long ... especially once you two actually do start your Trials."

Tannus froze as he considered the implications of Wren's words. "I'll just have to make sure I protect her," he said with newfound purpose.

"She doesn't need your protection," Wren insisted. "She needs both the strength and the actual desire to protect herself. I'm just not sure she'll be able to find it on her own. Not after whatever hard life she's had so far, and definitely not if she ends up Broken."

Tannus glanced back into the darkness of the mines. He could not bear to imagine losing yet another innocent friend to the savage cruelty of a world without mercy. "Just tell me what I need to do," he said sternly. And from that moment on, he committed himself to helping Dasia find all of the happiness that she deserved.

WANDERING FLICKERS OF gentle white light drifted slowly through the tunnels that afternoon as Tannus waited for Dasia to wake up. Transfixed by the hypnotic beauty of their effortless movements, he was reminded of the pale blue versions he had seen floating all around the Slumberwood tree only two nights before.

"What are they?" Tannus asked Wren during their modest midday meal.

"Just common wisps," Wren replied between bites. "They're all that's left when the spirits of people, or pets, or even wild animals are almost entirely out of Silver."

"Do they actually know we're here?" Tannus asked as one hovered mere inches above his head, circling as if to better understand the wild blond mane it had encountered. "Or do they just sorta ... float around and go wherever the wind blows?"

"I guess that depends on the wisp," Wren said with a shrug. "Some just try to stay near whatever source of Silver they can find. And others will stay near a person or place they knew while they were still alive. But these are all here 'cause of me."

"What do you mean?" Tannus asked with surprise, ever so tempted to swat away the one still circling.

"These are white wisps, so their spirits must've been aligned toward Asterlight while they were still alive—or, well, *more* alive. And since like attracts like, they always end up findin' their way to me."

"Are they dangerous?" Tannus asked as one slowly approached the tip of his nose.

"Not in small numbers. At most, they'll just try to steal a little bit of Silver from you when you're not lookin', and most people wouldn't even notice if they did. But if the entire swarm felt threatened, then you'd be surprised how much Silver they can steal in just a few minutes."

"Great," Tannus grumbled, disappointed he could not safely smack away the nearest one. "Why aren't any of 'em goin' near Dasia?"

"Probably 'cause she's got too much Frostwater in her veins," Wren said with a shrug. "As a general rule, most spirits try to stay away from anyone with a really cold or chaotic soul, and for good reason. You see, Frostwater's dangerous 'cause it can drain whatever Silver a spirit's got left, and Stormspark scares 'em 'cause too much can actually make a spirit explode."

"Whoa, cool!" Tannus gleefully replied, earning a disapproving buzz from the nearest wisp. "Oh, um ... sorry."

"Honestly, that's not even the weirdest part," said Wren. "Even though most spirits try to stay away from Frostwater, that's usually the only spectral element they'll leave behind wherever they go. Ms. Rondles said that's why haunted places are always so cold, and why so many people get ghostbumps whenever they're around. Oh! But if you wanna see somewhere *really* cool, there's this one place out here you two should check out as soon as you get the chance."

Reaching into a nearby satchel, Wren searched frantically for several moments, leaving Tannus to watch with amused anticipation.

"Ah, here we are," Wren announced before unrolling a hand-drawn map for Tannus to see. "It's called High Falls. You'll find it all the way out here, right on the edge of the Midwood Ridge. I've heard it's the most haunted place in Ranewood, and there are so many spirits who live there that the cliffs are covered in ice all year round. It's easily one of the prettiest spots out here … which is actually kinda sad when you stop and think about it."

Nodding intently while he listened, Tannus tried to memorize as much of the map as he could before Wren abruptly began to roll it up.

"Nice try," Wren said with a grin. "It wouldn't really be fair if I let you see all the other stuff that's out here before you've even started your Trials, now, would it?"

"Yeah, I'm pretty sure I rode an Ildarhorse right past 'fair' as soon as I decided to run around out here with her," Tannus replied. "Oh, and let's not forget this little problem." Then he opened one hand just long enough to conjure a tiny spectral flame.

It was their shared laughter that finally caused Dasia to stir from her hours-long rest.

"You two talk really loud," she grumbled. "And shouldn't one of you be watchin' the door?"

"Her Majesty will be pleased to hear that some of my little glowin' friends are keepin' a close eye on the woods," said Wren. "So as soon as they see a Cynder, I promise they'll let us know."

"Actually, speakin' of Cynders," said Tannus. "I've been meanin' to ask you … What's the deal with their faces? Right before we got attacked by Reinn and all his weirdo friends, they all started to look kinda like—"

"Monsters," Dasia interrupted, the terrifying memories still very much haunting her waking thoughts.

"It's just an illusion," Wren answered. "But most of 'em don't do it on purpose. The Ildarwood just has a way of makin' people look on the outside the way their souls do on the inside. For some, it's a gift. For others, it's a curse."

Dasia's mouth fell open with astonishment. "Would they still look like that outside these woods?"

"Well, most Cynders end up Broken before they fully finish their Trials," said Wren. "But if any of 'em did sneak out before that happened, the illusion wouldn't last for very long. Not unless they really knew what they were doin'. The world out there is just too different from the world in here. And the more time Ildarbound spend outside these woods, the weaker we get till we come back. In fact, that's mostly what these bracers are for, and why most Ildarbound don't even bother sneakin' home till their Trials are done."

"My gram told me she sometimes misses livin' out here," said Tannus. "I even asked her once if she'd ever want to come back. She said she'd love to, but since she wasn't a Preceptor anymore, the woods wouldn't let her stay for very long."

"Your grandmother's right," said Wren. "Once someone's Trials are over, their connection to the Ildarwood is supposed to be broken. That's the only safe way to ensure they can never come back and interfere in future Trials. The Principal Preceptor can make exceptions for other Preceptors and people who don't mind spendin' the rest of their lives in these woods. But for everyone else, the more time they spend in here, the weaker their souls will get until they leave."

"No wonder that Asterguard wasn't able to use Frostwater after you threw all that Goldenfire at him," said Dasia. "He must've been out here too long."

"My mom and dad used to say the Ildarwood wouldn't exist if not for the dreams of children," said Wren. "This place is supposed to be our safe haven. Our escape from the outside world. It'd be hard to escape long enough to find our own way through life if everyone out there could just come in here and screw everythin' up whenever they wanted."

Tannus could not help but laugh at Wren's uniquely colorful conclusion, and the added sight of Dasia actually smiling was enough to fill his heart with joy.

"Here, why don't you have somethin' to eat?" Wren offered, opening their satchel for Dasia. "I've got some dried fruit and a loaf of stale bread. Not the best options, I know, but it's not exactly easy to make it all the way to Westwatch and back with that much snow out there."

"Etta mentioned Westwatch right after she found us," recalled Tannus. "She said it's some sort of outpost."

"Yep. And it's the only one in this part of the woods," said Wren. "Most of the grown-ups who live out here have shops there. Plus there's a library, a Silverward, and the Principal Preceptor's office. Which reminds me—Delaniya Brent is one of the scariest ladies you'll ever meet, so just try to avoid her as much as you can your first year."

"We'll try," Tannus and Dasia replied at once, each one smirking at the other before noticing a sudden shift in the movement of all the wisps above their heads.

"Oh, that can't be good," said Tannus.

"It's not," Wren said with a sigh. "The Cynders must've found us."

"Okay, so now what do we do?" Tannus asked as Wren began to immediately pack up their supplies.

"You two will need to escape through one of the rear tunnels," Wren instructed before tossing a small pouch toward Tannus. "And you might as well take these with you."

"Um, what are they?" Tannus asked after a very brief inspection of the colorless crystals kept inside.

"Empty throwin' stones. They grow along the walls in some of the deepest parts of the mine. Fill 'em with Goldenfire as soon as you find someplace safe to set up camp. Then give some of 'em to her. That way, you can both fight fire with fire the next time any of these Cynders cross your path."

"Wait, what about you?" Dasia asked desperately. "Aren't you comin' with us?"

Wren shook their head and said, "If the Cynders were able to find us here, then it probably means they were able to follow some sort of trail … maybe some tracks in the snow, or even just a little bit of Silver from your wound. Either way, they're not gonna stop till they find you, so I'm gonna need to slow 'em down."

"But there's, like, twelve of 'em," said Tannus. "You'll never be able to fight that many off without our help."

"I wouldn't be able to fight that many off *with* your help, so why put you two at risk? Besides, I don't need to beat 'em. I just need to keep 'em busy long enough for you two to sneak away. After that, I can just duck into the deeper mines and wait for 'em to get tired of lookin' for me. And try not to worry. This isn't my first time playing howlin' hunters with a pack of Cynders."

"But … but … how are we supposed to find our way out?" asked Dasia, compelling Wren to face her one last time.

"Just follow Tannus. He'll know exactly where to go." Then Wren ran off into the darkness, a small swarm of wisps following close behind.

Tannus glanced back into the deeper tunnels, his eyes frantically searching for any signs of his old friend Fynn. Only once he had spotted the boy's ghostly face in the distance did he finally know which way to run.

A veritable maze awaited the two weary children as they raced to escape the pursuing Cynders. Ever careful to avoid wrong turns, unexpected falls, and slippery slopes, Tannus pulled Dasia through near-total darkness with little more than a minuscule flame in his palm to light the way.

Not until they had spotted daylight at last did they dare to breathe a long-awaited sigh of relief.

"I hope Wren's okay," Dasia said between breaths once they emerged outside, her attention turning back toward the snow-covered entrance to the long-abandoned mine.

"I'm sure they will be," Tannus offered, even as he feared what the Cynders might have done to the brave Anderen.

THERE WAS NO time to rest that afternoon as Tannus and Dasia trudged through feet of snow in the wooded hills of Miner's Reach. Desperate to find any form of shelter from the bitter cold, they marched past frozen ravines and enormous boulders, through open glades and long stretches of thick brush, until they emerged at last on the outermost edge of an abandoned settlement. Nestled inconspicuously in a narrow valley surrounded on all sides by trees and rock, the crumbling ruins seemed the perfect place for the two exhausted travelers to hide out, even if only for one night.

Far off in the distance, Tannus could already glimpse the towering stone cliffs of the fabled Midwood Ridge. Over one hundred feet high, even at their lowest point, they had served as a natural barrier for thousands of years, keeping first-year Ildarbound from wandering too far into the forest's dangerous depths. At least, so said his gram.

"Let's see if any of these places are safe enough for us to make camp for the night," Tannus suggested, making sure to survey the surroundings for any subtle signs of danger.

"What do you think happened here?" asked Dasia, her troubled eyes moving from one collapsing house to another. With generations of thick, knotted vines crawling up them, and heavy blankets of pristine snow piled upon their crumbling roofs, they were relics of a bygone era, long forgotten by those who had once called them home.

"If I had to guess ... probably the Astyrians," Tannus replied. And with every step he took, he became more convinced he could still hear the terrified cries of all who had once suffered in the midst of those long-abandoned structures.

"What about in there?" Dasia suggested, a single intact cottage catching her eye at the end of a narrow alley.

Tannus shuddered as he gazed upon it. No different from any of the other houses in design, it had a strange aura about it, leaving Tannus with the distinct impression that something terrible had once taken place within those very walls.

"I think we should keep lookin'," he suggested, even as Dasia continued walking toward it.

"All the other houses are cavin' in, so can't we at least take a quick look inside this one?"

Tannus huffed and grumbled, but he could see no suitable alternatives anywhere nearby. "Okay, fine," he conceded. "But let me go in first."

A simple door with no lock was all that stood between the elements outside and the dark tranquility of the room within. What few pieces of furniture still remained had been blackened by spectral fire, and broken dishes littered the dust-covered floor. All the paintings on the walls had long ago faded, and their frames were left crooked or otherwise damaged by events unknown.

No other rooms were there to discover within the tiny abode—not even a small bathroom they could use to wash up. Only a small, hidden closet did Tannus find, nestled away in the back, its door left open by whoever had used it last.

"It's not much," said Tannus. "But it's dry, and we should be able to keep it warm." Then he reached into his cloak pocket and retrieved the small jar with two Candlewood sticks still sealed within. "I'll need to find some scrap Ildarwood to light. Why don't you just lie down to rest while I go out and look?"

The words had barely left his mouth when Dasia collapsed onto the floor—this time, of her own accord.

"Hey, what's wrong? Are you okay?" Tannus asked urgently as he knelt beside her.

"This is all my fault," she said as tears cascaded down her cheeks. "My mom and dad were right. All I ever do is ruin people's lives."

"They actually said that to you?" Tannus said with astonishment, mortified beyond words that any parents would ever dare utter such hateful words.

"Yep. And they were right. I mean, look at what happened to them, and Demy, and Dustane. Then poor Etta probably got in trouble for lettin' us get away, and after that, you almost got blown up by Reinn!"

Tannus winced at the implication. "I'd like to think I was actually holdin' my own against him," he said, but Dasia was not at all amused.

"What about Wren? If they didn't get away, then whatever happened to them is all because of me too."

Tannus's heart broke as he struggled to think of anything he could say to bring Dasia even a single moment of comfort. "You can't keep blamin' yourself for everythin'," he reminded her. "Sometimes bad stuff just happens, even to good people. Like, neither one of us could pick our mom and dad. And if that Mimicus had come to my gram's house, I probably would've gotten fooled by it too. Plus, *I'm* the one who convinced *you* to stay out here, and I trusted those Cynders just as much as you. And I was also the one who found Wren, so really, it seems like there's more than enough blame here to go around."

Dasia's breaths fluttered as she shook her head. "I just can't do this anymore. It's not worth it. I mean, haven't you ever just wanted to give up and stop hopin' that things will ever get better?"

And for one brief moment, Tannus strongly considered telling the truth. But the longer he stared down at Dasia, the more clearly he could see the much braver version of himself that was reflected in her eyes. Far from the angry, defeated one he had seen in his gram's old mirror every day, it somehow seemed a great deal stronger and more heroic than he had ever imagined himself to be—so much so, in fact, that it actually gave him hope.

"Not while I've still got somethin' left to fight for," he said finally. "And right now, that's you. But whether you believe it yet or not, *I* know you're worth it."

Tannus found himself entirely unprepared for the sobbing that followed as Dasia flung her arms around him, hugging him harder than he had ever been hugged before. "I promise we're gonna be okay, no matter what," he told her. And it was a promise he intended to keep.

Tannus spent the rest of the day watching the forest for signs of danger after that, though only once a fire was lit and Dasia was as comfortable as could be in her makeshift bed.

Alert even as darkness returned to the forest, he found himself glancing back at her time and again to ensure none of her crippling fears or lingering self-doubts had suddenly returned.

Taking a seat beside her not long after midnight, Tannus finally allowed himself to breathe a long-awaited sigh of relief. *I just hope Wren was right*, he mused, ever wishful that the Cynders would not continue their hunt so late at night.

He had barely lain down beside Dasia before a subtle glimmer in the air caught his eye. Thinking it little more than a windswept speck of snow or dust at first, he allowed his gaze to linger in the seemingly empty space above Dasia as she slept. And a few seconds later, another glimmer appeared. Then one more.

His heart sank as he leaned forward, breathless with fear. Staring down at Dasia's cloak, he could see an almost invisible stream of spectral energy flowing ever so slowly through the fabric before drifting outside through the closed front door.

"Lost Silverblood will always find its way back to whichever soul caused it to flow," Tannus could recall his mother saying, not long after a bully at school had made him cry. "That's why you should *never* waste your tears on anyone who's gone and hurt you. You hear me? 'Cause all that ever does is make 'em stronger. And we don't want that, now, do we?"

"No," Tannus whispered, a familiar fire growing somewhere deep inside.

With renewed determination, he reached into the tiny pouch he had been given by Wren and firmly gripped a handful of colorless crystals in one hand. And by the time he finally opened his fingers, every throwing stone he held had been filled with a shimmering golden substance.

Tannus had made up his mind. The Cynders needed to be stopped, even if he needed to sacrifice himself in the process.

TANNUS AWAKENED AT dawn the next morning, just as soon as the first golden rays of sunshine poured in through the crumbling home's Ildarglass window.

"Where are you goin'?" Dasia asked, waking just in time to catch him sneaking outside.

"I'm gonna go look for more wood and try to find us a new place to stay," said Tannus. "I'll be back in a few hours, but I left you some throwin' stones, just in case. And if you see anyone outside you don't trust, just hide behind that secret door in the wall till I come back, okay?"

"You will come back, though, right?" Dasia asked with a smile. But in her eyes, Tannus could see the true desperation behind her question.

"I promise," he said, smiling back. His only hope in that moment was that he would be able to keep his word.

An almost invisible trail of Silver specks was all Tannus needed to find his way through the Ildarwood that morning. With dawn still fresh on the horizon, he chased the sparkling stream as it meandered up hills and down into narrow, snow-filled glens.

It did not take long for him to arrive atop a high ledge not far from the Cynders' cabin. He could even see well-worn tracks through the snow where their patrols had marched time and again once the days-long blizzard had finally cleared.

Sneaking through thick brush to avoid leaving an obvious trail, Tannus did not emerge until he was close enough to the Cynders' tracks to make use of them himself. He doubted Quill and her friends would ever be able to discern his footprints from their own. And from that remote spot, he ever so carefully made his way to a small grove, which stood barely a stone's throw away from one side of the hidden cabin.

Trembling nervously in the cold, Tannus reached into his cloak pocket and retrieved the few golden crystals he had brought with him. The sight of them alone was enough to send an invigorating surge of energy flowing throughout his shivering body. Imagining the chaos that would ensue once the cabin erupted into Goldenfire flames, he could not wait to watch all the Cynders finally experience true justice.

"Don't," a soft voice whispered from behind, catching Tannus so entirely by surprise that he nearly dropped the crystals into the snow.

"Fynn?" Tannus gasped, amazed to see the spirit of his friend mere inches away. "What do you mean, don't? Why not?"

No further words did the spirit speak that morning, for so little strength did he have left. Instead, he merely reached out to touch Tannus's face, sending a surge of memories racing through his head.

Flashes of a raging fire exploded instantly into view. A night that had haunted his dreams for over a year, suddenly brought to life in terrifying detail. The screams of Fynn's parents and siblings as they begged the Heavens for someone to save him from the flames. The cheers of all the golden monsters standing in a circle around the house, their faces distorted by the corruption and hatred in their souls. The fear that left Fynn paralyzed as he hid. The agony of all the members of the city's fire watch who had to search the rubble for Fynn and Tannus both. The sorrow of Fynn's family and Tannus's own gram as they wept over the two boys in the Silverward the next day.

Fynn vanished in an instant once the soul-crushing stream of memories finally ended, leaving Tannus shaking and breathless in the snow.

"Fynn? Fynn?" he whispered desperately, finding only a single frail wisp floating away in the breeze. "Fynn …"

Tears of Silver fell from Tannus's face as he knelt in the grove and struggled to clear his head. Like so many times before, the vengeance he had so desperately craved was just within reach. Yet because of Fynn's unexpected intervention, Tannus could no longer muster the fury he needed to proceed.

"No, I can't turn into one of them," he insisted. "There has to be some other way."

Only then did the remnant wisp begin to circle and bob in a single spot, as if to draw Tannus's eye. Sneaking over to it on his hands and knees, Tannus focused on the seemingly empty air where the remains of Fynn's spirit still lingered. It took Tannus several long moments to notice a pale blue glimmer flowing ever so slowly in his direction. Then another. Then one more. Barely even visible, the sparkling flecks created a trail, not from Dasia but from someone else—someone Tannus himself had injured just enough to leave them with an almost imperceptible spectral wound of their own.

Tannus gasped the instant he realized who that was.

Racing west back toward town, Tannus made sure to keep his steps within the well-worn tracks left behind by other travelers. He did not dare stop for rest until he spotted a familiar face out on patrol. Wearing scorched blue armor made of Ildarglass, the Asterguard named Garson Leck had enlisted four new Ildarwulves in his search for Tannus and Dasia, making it all too clear to Tannus just how determined the man was not to let them slip through his fingers again.

"This ought to be fun," Tannus whispered before taking a deep breath and covering his face as best he could. Then he leaped up from the spot where he hid and shouted in a deep and angry voice. "Hey, you big blue dolt! You better head back to town right now, or I'm gonna get all my scary Cynder friends to come out here and show you who *really* runs these woods!"

And before the Asterguard could even react, Tannus threw his meager supply of golden crystals toward him and watched them soar through the air with unnatural speed. Exploding on contact with a patch of Ildarwood trees mere feet away from where the Asterguard stood, they released so much more Goldenfire than Tannus had expected that he fell backward with surprise.

"You little brat!" the Asterguard shouted from the massive pile of snow he had leaped into.

"Consider that your only warnin'!" Tannus yelled back before running for his life.

Within seconds, four terrifying Ildarwulves had begun their hunt while their irate master shouted for help from other Asterguards nearby.

And so the race was on!

Tannus knew he could not stay ahead of the Ildarwulves for long, though for once in his short life, he actually found himself grateful that the snow around him was so deep. Unable to run with the same lightning speed they might otherwise have as an advantage, the four unleashed creatures would need time to forge their own paths—crucial minutes Tannus was counting on to complete the rest of his ill-conceived plan.

Sprinting as fast as his legs could carry him, he needed only a single glance back at the pursuing Ildarwulves to know his time was running out. But with the Cynders' cabin at last in sight, and no Ildarstar in place to protect it from unwanted guests, there was nothing stopping Tannus from paying his old friends a rather quick and unexpected visit.

Bursting through the door, much to the surprise of all within, Tannus shouted, "I hope you guys have room for four more!" Then he sprinted out through the back door before promptly closing it behind him.

Seconds later, mayhem ensued as four eager Ildarwulves leaped inside the house and began entangling as many Cynders as they could catch. Cursing and explosions followed as the Cynders fought desperately to break themselves free. Their efforts would be in vain, for within minutes, a swarm of Asterguards converged swiftly upon them.

Flashes of emerald, sapphire, and gold reflected off the pure white snow as a ferocious battle ensued, leaving Tannus to watch with glee as the Cynders were captured one by one. The very last of them to surrender was Reinn, who was nearly frozen solid by the time two Asterguards had finally carried him out of the house.

Tannus could not have been more proud of himself. Somehow his plan had actually worked!

A long, cold walk followed as he made his way back to the abandoned settlement where he and Dasia had last found shelter. Making sure to gather some Ildarwood branches along the way, he was excited beyond words to tell her what he had done. After two long, miserable days, they would finally be safe.

"Hey, Dasia. You'll never guess what happened," he announced upon entering the old house, a pile of firewood in his arms. "Dasia? Where the heck did you go?"

But much to his surprise, Dasia was nowhere to be found.

Staring down at the spot where she had slept, Tannus found her supplies still piled neatly where she had left them, and her winter cloak was still hanging from its hook.

"Somethin' is not right," Tannus whispered, desperate to find out where she had gone and why she had left. Glancing at the rickety old door to the house, he needed only an instant to realize it was made from solid Ildarwood.

Never, ever try to see memories from any Ildarwood unknown … not unless you're willing to pay a truly terrible price.

His father's words echoed in his mind as Tannus approached the door's sparkling surface. There was no telling what unspeakable horrors the door had seen in the untold decades since the house had been built, yet if he wanted to find out what had happened to Dasia, he would most certainly need to risk experiencing all those tragic memories himself.

Placing his bare hand against the door, Tannus closed his eyes and tried to remember his father's lessons. "Please just show me what happened to Dasia," he whispered. Then distant screams gave way to momentary flashes of heart-wrenching scenes from far darker times.

Tannus refused to surrender to his fear and held on to the door for dear life. Only after what felt to him like a brief eternity did he finally glimpse the memories he had so desperately sought. And by the time he was done, he could hardly believe what he had seen.

Reflections of the Past

A BONE-CHILLING BREEZE SNUCK in through the walls that
morning while Dasia waited patiently for Tannus. Yet much to
her surprise, neither an extra blanket nor moving closer to the fire was
enough to keep her warm.

"*Dasia*," a gentle voice whispered from somewhere outside, causing
ghostbumps to surge up and down her arms.

"Tannus?" Dasia said nervously, rising from her seat and glancing out through one of the home's few windows. Yet nothing but the
snow-covered settlement could she see.

"*Dasia, please …*" the voice whispered from beyond the door.

Dasia froze. Who else but Tannus could possibly know she was
there?

Hesitant to open the door, Dasia pressed her ear against it and listened carefully for any clear sounds on the other side.

"*Please let me in,*" said the voice, sending chills down Dasia's
spine.

"Demy?" she asked between panicked breaths, too afraid to believe that her beloved brother had truly returned. "No. You're not my brother," she insisted, turning away from the door and focusing solely on the warmth of the crackling spectral fire.

"*Dasia, please ...*" the voice repeated. "*I came to warn you ...*"

Dasia turned back toward the door. "Warn me about what?"

"*Tannus ...*"

"Tannus what? What happened to Tannus?" Dasia asked with alarm.

"*Tannus is gone ...*"

Dasia gasped as her stomach churned. "You're just tryin' to trick me," she said firmly, despite her deepening fears. "How am I supposed to know if you're tellin' the truth?"

Silence followed, leaving Dasia to grow more anxious with each passing second.

"Demy? Demy, are you still there?" she asked, but there was no answer.

So once again, she took a few steps toward the door and pressed her ear against its sparkling surface. This time, however, there were neither words nor whispers to hear.

Dasia took a deep breath, then opened the door with utmost caution. At once, a frigid breeze surged inside, briefly troubling the spectral fire. Yet no matter where outside she looked, no one and nothing stood there waiting.

"I've missed you, Dasia."

A brief scream followed as Dasia turned to find the ghostly visage of Demitris standing behind her.

"I'm so sorry. I didn't mean to scare you," the spirit offered, both hands held out innocently in front of him.

"Demy? Is it really you this time?" Dasia asked as tears welled up in her eyes. Struggling to catch her breath after the jarring fright, she so desperately wanted to believe that the spirit standing before her was in fact the brother she had lost so long ago.

"It's really me, but I can't stay for long," said the spirit. "I've come to warn you. Tannus is gone."

"What do you mean, gone?" Dasia asked suspiciously. "Where did he go?"

"He lied about goin' to look for a safe place to stay. He really went to go attack the Cynders. He didn't want 'em to hurt you ever again. But then he got caught, and now …"

"Now what?" Dasia demanded as her heart beat faster.

"The Cynders … they Broke him, Dasia. So now he's never comin' back."

A sudden numbness left Dasia breathless. Her worst nightmare had once again come true—yet another life ruined because of her.

"No … I … you're just tryin' to trick me. I mean … no, that just can't be true," Dasia managed as she slowly fell to pieces on the floor beside the fire. "What am I supposed to do now?"

The spirit knelt beside her and shook his head with deep remorse. "There's only one thing you can do, Dasia. Just come with me, and I promise, I'll make sure no one can ever hurt you again."

"What do you mean?" asked Dasia, one hand wiping the pale blue tears from her pallid cheeks. "Where would we go?"

"Somewhere we can be together forever."

Dasia stared up into the eyes that looked so very much like those of her beloved older brother. And though every fiber of her being warned her that the spirit should not be trusted, she had grown so incredibly tired of all the loneliness and pain that had plagued her life for so very long that she simply could not imagine living with it anymore.

"Okay," she finally conceded. "I'm ready."

Stepping out into the snow without her cloak or any supplies, Dasia took a deep breath. She could still see all the footprints in the snow that Tannus had left not long before. "I'm sorry, Tannus," she whispered.

A somber silence followed as she followed the ghostly image of Demitris due north toward the Midwood Ridge.

It did not take them long to reach a scene of such idyllic winter beauty that Dasia stood breathless at first sight of it. Hundreds of feet high, the cascading currents of the falls before her seemed to emerge from the Heavens themselves before plunging into a sparkling pool of cerulean water. A prismatic mist lingered perpetually in the air, while all along the sheer granite cliffs, pale blue ice formed into enormous dangling spears.

Along the water's edge, frozen sheets had formed with lingering snowfall covering their surfaces. And dancing here and there all around the trees and flowing waters were colorful wisps of different sizes, each one seemingly unaware that there were suddenly guests in their midst.

"What is this place?" Dasia asked with wonder.

"It's called High Falls," the apparition answered with a smile. "This is where the spirits of almost all the lost children in Ranewood eventually end up. That way, they never have to be alone again. Isn't it pretty?"

"It's incredible," Dasia replied, unable to believe the sheer splendor before her.

"We don't ever have to leave. We can stay here forever. And we'll never have to worry about Mom and Dad bein' mean to us ever again. Wouldn't that be great?"

It all sounded so peaceful, and in a way, even better than anything else she could have hoped for after a year of misery at home. "What do I have to do?" she asked the spirit.

"Just come with me."

The apparition wasted no time leading Dasia over to the water's edge, then he beckoned her to follow him out onto the snow-covered ice.

Reluctant at first, Dasia began to envision Demitris falling through the ice of Lake Abalus one year before. She could even hear him crying out into the night as he so desperately thrashed while trying to escape.

"I ... I'm not sure."

"Dasia, please," the spirit insisted. "I'm so lonely without you."

Dasia took a few steps forward. Then the familiar sound of a single crack forming in the ice echoed out against the cliffs.

"Just a few more steps," said the spirit.

"Won't it hurt?" Dasia asked nervously.

"Only for a minute. Then you'll never feel any pain ever again."

Dasia took another two steps forward, then a second loud *crack* echoed out into the woods. "I'm so scared," she whispered as her entire body began to tremble.

"Just look at me," said the spirit, "and I promise it'll all be over soon."

One more reluctant step forward, and Dasia stood perilously close to the rushing water's edge.

"You're almost there," said the spirit, a proud, loving smile upon his face.

"*I wouldn't do that if I were you,*" a soft voice sang from somewhere in the trees along the bank.

Dasia swiftly spun around to find its source. Several agonizing moments passed before she finally spotted a shy little girl with bright red hair hiding behind a sparkling trunk.

"Who are you?" Dasia asked through shivering lips.

"My name's Rosie. Who are you?" the little girl replied.

Dasia froze. "I'm … um … You know, you really shouldn't be out here all by yourself. Where are your mom and dad?"

But instead of answering right away, the little girl ducked behind the nearest tree, then reappeared an instant later behind another several feet away. "They went away a long time ago," she said somberly. "So now I just live here."

A wave of ghostbumps ran up and down Dasia's arms. "Do you like it here?" she asked nervously. "Are you happy?"

The little girl hid behind another tree before leaping out from behind a third. "People come here all the time," she answered. "Sometimes they leave. Sometimes they don't. But then other people come, and they're all really, really sad."

Dasia's breaths hastened as she glanced back at the apparition of her brother.

"Don't listen to her, Dasia," said the ghostly Demitris. "Listen to me. I'm your brother, and I love you, and I just want to save you from years of sufferin' while I still have the chance. Now, please … just come to me."

"He's just tryin' to trick you," the little girl sang, causing another stabbing pain in Dasia's stomach.

"Argh, useless wretch!" the false Demitris shouted, his eyes lighting up with fury before he vanished and reappeared precisely where the little girl had once stood.

"Hey! Leave her alone!" Dasia commanded, but the sinister spirit had grown tired of their little game. Turning back towards Dasia, his face began to take on a vaguely monstrous visage.

"Wanna see somethin' cool?" he said with a grin, causing Dasia to gasp with surprise. Then the spirit shot forward with unnatural speed before passing directly through Dasia, knocking her backward into the ice-cold waters beneath the falls.

Shock immediately set in, leaving Dasia gasping for air as she struggled to stay afloat. "Help! Please, somebody help!" she screamed, while mere feet away, the monstrous version of her brother laughed and relished every intoxicating ounce of her suffering.

"Isn't this what you wished for, Dasia?" the false Demitris asked mockingly. "Isn't this what you thought you really deserved after what you did?"

Dasia could feel the final remnants of life slipping away from her, body and soul. And as she slipped beneath the surface, brokenhearted and alone, her final thoughts were of her brothers, her parents, and of Tannus.

"Dasia!"

That was the last word she heard as one final breath escaped, her heart desperately wishing for only one more chance at life.

She could not see the face of the person who pulled her from the water seconds later, but she found immediate comfort in the radiating heat that flowed from their fingers, through her lifeless arms, and into her aching soul.

The next thing she knew, she was being dragged onto the icy shore as she most desperately gasped for air.

"What the heck is wrong with you?" Tannus demanded, taking off his cloak without a second thought and frantically using it to dry her off. "Have you lost your mind?"

Yet so paralyzed with exhaustion was Dasia that the only words she could manage in response were "Look out!"

Eager to claim another victim, the false spirit of Demitris charged directly through Tannus, knocking the wind out of him and sending him tumbling backwards into the frigid waters beneath High Falls.

"Tannus, no!" Dasia cried out, but there was nothing she could do. Her legs and arms had lost all feeling. She had barely any strength left with which to move. Sparkling tears cascaded down her cheeks as she was forced to watch her only friend in the entire world slowly succumb to the exact same fate as the real Demitris.

"It hurts, doesn't it?" the false Demitris mocked. "Having to watch it happen all over again and knowing their deaths are all your fault. First Demitris. Then Dustane. Now Tannus. But now it can all finally end with you."

Yet out of everything the false Demitris had said, only a single name stood out.

Suddenly compelled to crawl forward, Dasia dragged herself toward the water, inch by excruciating inch, as the false Demitris savored every tantalizing drop of Silver that he had earned from his victims' suffering.

"You can't save him, and you can't save yourself, so you might as well just give up," he told her with a laugh as she reached the water's edge.

Barely able to focus, Dasia stared at Tannus, who desperately struggled to stay afloat just out of reach. That was when she knew for certain that the false Demitris was right. She could not save Tannus, and she could not save herself. All she could do in that most dire of moments was surrender—just not in the way that the cruel apparition had intended.

Staring down at her reflection in the water, Dasia began to see Dustane's frightened face staring back at her. "I'm so sorry," she said as pale blue tears fell from her cheeks down onto the ghostly reflection. "I never should have let them lock you away."

With the very last of her strength, Dasia reached out and touched the troubled waters. And for one brief instant, she truly believed that she could feel his ice-cold fingers touching hers.

"You deserve to be free," she whispered. They were her final words.

An almost invisible shock wave exploded through the Ildarwood as Dasia perished, sending the Mimicus soaring backward and knocking Tannus several feet beneath the water's surface.

Desperate to take one final breath, Tannus forced himself to swim up toward the surface with the very last remnants of his strength. Gasping for air the instant his head finally emerged from beneath the frigid depths, he glimpsed a mysterious figure standing on the water's edge. Then Tannus watched with disbelief as pale blue ice began to form a sturdy bridge between them.

Dragged up out of the water, Tannus could barely believe his eyes. The face staring down at him looked so very familiar, yet somehow forever changed.

"Dasia?" Tannus managed.

"Dasia's gone," the boy replied. "My name's Dustane."

"You won't be able to save him," the false Demitris called out from the forest, visibly weakened by the blast and barely able to maintain his boyish visage. "The cold will kill you both before anyone even realizes you're here."

But Dustane was unconvinced. Determined to save his freezing friend, Dustane searched the cloak Tannus had taken off only minutes before. And from its pocket he retrieved a small jar, which still contained a single radiant stick made of Candlewood.

"This should help keep you warm," Dustane said before placing the Candlewood remnant in Tannus's trembling hands. It took mere seconds for the intense spectral warmth to flow through him entirely, body and soul.

Only then did Dustane finally turn toward the false spirit of his brother. All he needed was a single icy glare to freeze the Mimicus where it stood.

"Wanna see somethin' cool?" Dustane asked with a grin, recalling the lessons he had learned from both Tannus and the real Demitris. Then he reached one hand out toward the cerulean pool beneath the falls and began to summon a shimmering stream of Frostwater directly toward him. Channeling it slowly up one arm and out through the other, he threw his left hand forward and released a powerful surge of spectral ice, which collided with the awestruck spirit like a raging river full of sleet.

Drained of all his remnant energy, the ruthless Mimicus dissipated into a fine spectral mist, never to be seen or heard from again.

Utterly exhausted by the whole ordeal, Dustane fell to his knees, then managed one final smile before finally collapsing onto the ice beside Tannus.

And so they waited there together, side by side in the frigid cold, each one desperately hoping for rescue. Two souls forever changed by the encounter.

Tannus and Dustane.

❖

SHIMMERING DROPS OF Silver fell gently from the ceiling for hours, down onto the two boys resting far below.

Not until late in the evening did Dustane finally stir within the ancient Silverward of Westwatch, his gaze immediately drawn to the tangle of Ildarwood roots directly above him. Only a single twisted tendril pointed down in his direction, its glowing tip releasing periodic doses of pure spectral energy—precisely what he needed to recover from his days-long ordeal.

"How are you feeling?" asked a woman at the foot of his bed. Wearing an imposing dress with absolutely no frills of any sort, the woman had dark brown skin, matching eyes, and a persistently stern expression.

"Wh-who are you?" Dustane nervously replied.

"My name is Delaniya Brent. I'm the town's Principal Preceptor, which means I'm responsible for the well-being of every child that enters these woods … Ildarbound or not."

A sudden knot formed in Dustane's stomach. "What happened to Tannus?" he dared to ask the imposing woman.

"Your friend will be just fine," said Delaniya, one finger pointing toward the sleeping boy in an adjacent bed. "You have no idea how lucky you are that Etta found you when she did. A few minutes longer, and there's no telling how much permanent damage might have been done."

"I'm the lucky one," said Dustane, his attention solely on Tannus. "He kept riskin' his life to save me, even when he didn't really know who I was."

"Which brings me to my next question," Delaniya began before putting on a pair of wire-frame glasses and inspecting the small pile of papers on the table beside her. "According to my records, there were only two children reported missing in these woods: one was Tannus Ambers, and the other was called Anaesdasia Dulane. Dare I ask what happened to her?"

Dustane froze as he stared up at the woman, her penetrating gaze so utterly severe that he dared not lie. "Dasia's gone," he said finally. "My name's Dustane."

"I see," Delaniya promptly replied, one eyebrow rising only a hair. "This may come as a surprise, but your parents were not exactly forthcoming about your past when Overseer Brent and I first spoke with them. Thankfully, my counterpart in Marshwood was able to find your original record of birth. I'm sure you can imagine my surprise when it listed two different names: Anaesdasia Levasia Dulane, a girl, and Dustane Idanis Dulane, a boy. And according to that document, you two were spectral twins. Do you know what that means?"

Dustane hesitated. "That the two of us were born sharing a soul?"

"Spectral twins occur when two souls share one body," Delaniya clarified. "There's no such thing as two bodies sharing a soul. But I'm sure you already knew that, didn't you?"

Dustane slowly looked away with shame. There were few things he regretted more than all the half-truths he had shared with Tannus two nights before.

"I'm afraid there's more," said Delaniya, drawing Dustane's nervous gaze once again. "Upon closer inspection of the record, I discovered a hidden note from the attending Healer—a message that only another Healer or well-intentioned Preceptor could ever see."

"What did it say?" asked Dustane, his grip upon the bedsheets suddenly tightening.

"That your parents apparently lied to you and everyone else all along. You were never *truly* a spectral twin at all. No, you are what most people would call cross-spirited. In your case, that means you were born with the soul of a boy inside the body of a girl. And it is hardly uncommon. In fact, we tend to see it in roughly one out of a hundred births."

"I ... I don't understand," Dustane stammered. "My mom and dad have always said we had two *different* souls."

"There was *never* any other soul," Delaniya insisted. "As best I can tell, your mother and father had so desperately wanted a daughter that they convinced you, their doctor, and apparently themselves that you had an incredibly rare condition—one in which a pair of twinned souls end up fighting for control of a single body, often at the cost of one soul's life. But based on everything I've found, you have only ever been Dustane from the start."

"But ... why would they do that?" Dustane asked as his heart began to break.

"I'm afraid there are still some ... *misguided* people in this world who believe that such situations are unnatural, with more than a few who even go so far as to claim it's some sort of contagion or disease. But I can assure you here and now that it is none of those things. In fact, being born cross-spirited is no more an illness than having red hair instead of brown, or being left-handed instead of right. It's just another harmless way for the Heavens to make sure each and every person in the world is unique in their own special way."

"But if I didn't have two souls, then why did my mom and dad use a special door to keep my spirit locked away for years?"

Delaniya took a few steps forward before sitting on the side of Dustane's bed. Taking his hand gently in her own, she said, "Ildarwood can be used to do many incredible things ... and sometimes it can be used to do things that are truly terrible. Now, in genuine cases with spectral twins, the approach they used, though controversial, could be used to save the life of whichever soul is more likely to survive. However, in your case, it would appear that what they tried to lock away instead was just a single part of your soul—the part that quite simply wanted to look and act like most other boys. That way, they could try to convince whatever was left that you were a girl. I just wish I could say I've never heard of something like this happening before, but I'm afraid not all parents in this world are willing to accept that their child was born different. And in some rare cases, they might even go to extraordinary lengths in a desperate attempt to either change or conceal the truth."

Dustane could hardly believe his ears. So many years had he wasted utterly convinced that everything his parents did and said was part of a genuine effort to save their child's life. "I honestly thought there were two of us all along," he confessed, his eyes eager to avoid the Principal Preceptor's. "I even used to pretend that me and Dasia could actually talk to each other. I don't really know why. But now, lookin' back, I just feel so foolish."

"Sometimes, when we're feeling most afraid or all alone," said Delaniya, "we talk to ourselves as a way to cope, especially after years of trauma or abuse. In your case, I suspect you knew somewhere deep down inside that everything your mother and father were telling you was a lie, but you probably had all those conversations just in case there really *was* another spirit just as lonely as yours right on the other side of that locked door."

Sparkling tears cascaded down Dustane's cheeks as he considered the implications. Yet only then, as the resulting mists drifted away, did he finally notice his reflection in the small standing mirror beside the bed.

"Why do I look so different?" he asked with momentary awe, entirely surprised to see the boyish face staring back at him.

It was a question that very nearly made the unshakable Delaniya Brent crack a minuscule smile. "The Ildarwood has a unique way of making people look on the outside precisely the way they do on the inside. And I'm sure you'll be relieved to hear that, given enough time out here, your body will naturally correct itself until there's no longer any need for such illusions, even after your Trials are through. It's a truly fascinating process. One that typically only happens to people who are genuinely born cross-spirited."

Dustane's expression was filled with wonder as he stared at the version of himself he had secretly dreamed of for so long. But then an alarming fear leaped to the forefront of his mind. "Wait, does that mean I'll go back to looking like a girl tomorrow when I leave?"

Delaniya nodded her head solemnly. "I'm afraid so. The illusions of the Ildarwood don't usually persist outside the forest … at least, not without certain skills that can sometimes take years to master. But I may know someone who can help, so just leave it with me, and I'll see what I can do."

Dustane managed a weak smile of gratitude before daring to ask the two lingering questions he feared the answers to most of all. "So … what happens now? Will I have to go back home?"

"That is entirely up to you," said Delaniya. "From everything I've seen, I would hardly consider your mother and father fit parents, so I will certainly understand if you would prefer not to see them again. However, I have also seen cases where even the most dysfunctional families somehow found the strength and love they needed to heal their shared wounds together over time, with mutual consent and proper counsel—though such a process can often take years. More often than not, however, the divide is simply too great, and nothing we do can truly help either or both parents come to terms with whichever reality it is that they outright refuse to accept."

Dustane let out a heavy sigh as he considered both options. "Even if I *do* try to forgive 'em, I'm not really sure my mom and dad will ever be able to love me again. Not after everythin' I've done."

Delaniya Brent then stared at Dustane with unwavering determination. "Far too often our past is an anchor that holds us back, while hope is a light that guides us forward. We alone must choose which will win, the anchor or the light."

A momentary silence followed as Dustane struggled to find comfort in her wise words.

"You know what never ceases to amaze me?" Delaniya asked suddenly, her attention drifting toward the nearest window. "The incredible power of these woods. The way they can help a person discover their best possible self, or at times, reveal their worst. I've seen this forest affirm the greatest strengths of countless children and wash away their greatest flaws. And I've watched destinies change in the blink of an eye … sometimes just because two kindred spirits happened to find each other at precisely the right time."

Delaniya then stared back into Dustane's glistening eyes and said, "You may not know this, but when you were born, the attending Healer also noted that you emerged holding a sparkling amethyst stone, just like countless other souls aligned toward Kingswash before you. And in many cultures, that would be taken as a sign that you were destined to lead a passive life … one where you would always surrender to the whims of prevailing currents, forever willing to sacrifice your own comfort for the sake of maintaining the illusion of peace. That's why the motto for all such souls is 'Calm in raging tides.'

"But when I look at you now, the eyes staring back at me show no lingering signs of that type of person. No. What I see is the eyes of a survivor. A soul transformed by all the struggles it has long been forced to endure. Which is why it seems so fitting that your alignment has so drastically changed."

Surprised by the Preceptor's words, Dustane thought back to his brief encounter with the false Demitris near the frigid pool beneath High Falls. "I can control Frostwater now, can't I?" he asked with no small measure of reluctant pride.

"So it would seem," said Delaniya, "which means you must learn to live by a new motto: 'Endure any winter.' Seems rather fitting now, don't you think?"

Dustane managed a momentary grin as the Principal Preceptor maintained her rigid expression.

"If nothing else, remember this. You are not the person you once were," Delaniya said before standing to leave. "You have a whole new life ahead of you, so try not to let the shadows of the past keep you from enjoying a brighter future. You've fought so very hard to earn it. And so has he."

Dustane glanced over at Tannus once more. And though he was

relieved beyond words that they had both survived their harrowing ordeal at High Falls, he could not help but wonder if the boy who had so willingly risked his life to save Dasia would wake up still willing to be friends with Dustane.

Seeming to sense his inner angst, Delaniya Brent turned to face him one last time. "You know, there's one last thing I find fascinating," she said from beside the main Silverward doors. "What are the odds that a boy like Tannus, whose life was so irreparably upended by fire and rage, would happen to find himself lost in the woods with the perfect companion—a soul born aligned to tranquil waters and later transformed by the lingering chill of spectral frost? Someone might even be inclined to think that the Ildarwood itself actually wanted you two to meet."

It was a notion that left Dustane smiling widely, his heart filling with hope for the very first time.

IT WAS JUST past midnight when Tannus stirred at last, prompting Dustane to sit up swiftly with relief.

"It's about time you woke up," he told Tannus, who began to hold his own forehead with both hands.

"I feel like somebody ran me over with a carriage," Tannus grumbled, unable to focus his attention on anyone or anything. "Actually, make that two carriages." Only after a few moments of suffering did he finally turn and see Dustane. "What happened to you?" he asked with surprise, causing Dustane to look away.

For hours on end, Dustane had been rehearsing everything he wanted to say. But now that the time to explain had finally arrived, he found himself struggling to find the right words.

"It's a long story," he began, suddenly fearful of how Tannus might react.

"What's the short version?" asked Tannus, his discerning stare fixed solely on the boy in the nearby bed.

"My name's Dustane," he said nervously. "My mom and dad had me convinced I was someone I'm not, but this is the real me. The me I was always supposed to be."

Tannus remained silent for several moments as he maintained his unwavering stare. Yet every second he waited to reply felt like pure agony to Dustane.

"Please say somethin'," Dustane implored as his heart raced and his stomach churned.

"Is it okay if I call you Dustie?" asked Tannus, causing Dustane to gasp with surprise.

"Honestly, that sounds great," he replied as tears welled up in his eyes.

It was the first night in his entire life that he went to sleep feeling entirely like himself. And he could not possibly have been any happier.

A New Sun Rising

TANNUS AND DUSTANE awakened at dawn the next morning, just as soon as the first golden rays of sunshine poured in
through the stained-glass windows of the Westwatch Silverward. Glancing over at each other with cheerful grins, neither could have been more
thrilled to see the other smiling back.

"You know, I thought you two might get up early," Etta called out
from the main entrance, a raggedy old satchel slung over her shoulder.
"I hope yas don't mind, but I brought a mutual friend."

Following close behind, Wren beamed with joy upon seeing Tannus
and Dustane both alive and well.

"You two really had us worried," Etta confessed before taking a seat
between their beds. "But my goodness ... if anyone had told me the
two of yas were gonna get a whole pack of Cynders kicked out of these
woods after only two days, well ... I would've guessed they were either
drunk or had a really bad case of the sillies. Not to mention what yas
did to that awful Mimicus."

"The Cynders were all Tannus," said Dustane. "I just got really lucky with that spirit."

"Somethin' tells me luck had nothin' to do with it," said Etta. "I guess messin' with you is one mistake he won't ever make again."

"From the sounds of it, I don't think he'll be makin' any mistakes again," Wren said with amusement.

"We were really worried about you," said Dustane. "Were you able to get away from the Cynders without gettin' hurt?"

"They put up one heck of a fight," said Wren, "but I know those tunnels way better than they do, so I was able to find a safe place to hide before they did too much damage. Although Reinn really did a number on a lot of those poor wisps."

"I wouldn't feel too bad about that," said Etta. "I'm still convinced most of those little buggers used to be Astyrians, so good riddance."

"You'll have to forgive Etta. She sometimes forgets that all Selyrians are *supposed* to believe in the right of redemption."

"Oh, I'm sure they've all had just the right amount of redemption now," Etta said with a grin.

"So the Cynders all really got what they deserved?" Dustane asked cheerfully.

"They sure did," said Etta. "We've been lookin' for an excuse to kick the worst of 'em outta the Ildarwood for over a year, but we didn't really have a good reason till their entire pack decided to pick a fight with about half a dozen Asterguards. And since Ildarbound aren't allowed to attack any grown-ups in these woods, Principal Brent's hands were pretty much tied."

Needless to say, Tannus and Dustane could not have been more thrilled with the news.

"Oh! Before I forget," said Etta, one hand reaching into her satchel, "I brought a present for, um …"

"Dustane," Tannus and Dustane replied at once.

"Oh, Dustane, huh? I like it. You look a lot more like a Dustane," Etta said with a smile. Then she presented Dustane with a simple box made of sparkling gray Ildarwood. "I thought you might be needin' these before you go."

Dustane glanced at Tannus before daring to open the unexpected gift. Glimpsing within, he was surprised to discover hundreds of small red berries, each with crystalline sheens and a gentle glow. "Oh, wow, they're beautiful! But what are they?" he asked the old Preceptor.

"Seedless Ildarian yewberries," Etta proudly replied. "The greenwood variety has pits that are poisonous enough to put down a full-grown bear, but these right here are special. They come from a grove of crimson Yewwood trees, which only grow on the highest hills in the Ildarwood. Just eat one of these every night before bed, and you'll wake up lookin' exactly like you. That way, you won't have to wait till your Trials to see your real self in the mirror."

Dustane could hardly believe his ears, and he was so incredibly touched by the gift that he leaped out of his bed to give Etta a hug. His only disappointment was that he would need to wait a whole year before he could finally see her again.

A SMALL CROWD of Preceptors awaited Tannus and Dustane later that morning, just as soon as they emerged into the massive central hall of Westwatch Tower. Each boy took a moment to marvel at the beauty of the majestic Ranewood tree growing up from the center of the hall. With dangling amethyst leaves and sparkling glass-like flowers, all it needed was the slightest breeze to release a melodic chime so incredibly soothing that Tannus and Dustane both felt immediately calmed in its presence.

Waving goodbye to Etta and Wren, they joined the Principal Preceptor in her Ildarhorse-drawn carriage. Only a single unspoken command from Delaniya Brent did the two mighty steeds need before abruptly taking off.

It was a long, slow ride through the Ildarwood from the great market around Westwatch, for roads within the forest were few and far between. And once they emerged from a hidden entrance to the Ildarwood near the southernmost part of town, they made their way first to the cozy riverside cottage that Tannus had only briefly called home.

A familiar knot returned to his stomach as he stared out through the carriage window. Only a few weeks earlier, he had hated the mere thought of having to live with his old gram. Yet after his brief adventure in the Ildarwood, he suddenly found himself terrified beyond words that she might not want to take him back.

"I'm quite certain she'll understand," Delaniya offered, her expression just as stern as always despite the reassuring tone of her voice.

Tannus emerged from the carriage that morning with a lingering sense of sickness and dread. He could not stand the feeling that he had let his gram down, though at the exact same time, he knew from his father's stories just how angry she could sometimes get. But with Dustane standing proudly by his side, he suddenly found within himself all the strength he needed to proceed.

Three times did Delaniya knock upon the old woman's door before Gram finally answered. The next thing Tannus knew, he was being pulled into her bosom and hugged tighter than he had ever been hugged before.

"It's about time you came back! Oh, you have no idea how worried I've been," she said before finally releasing Tannus. Then she stared down at her grandson lovingly, only to thwack him once on the side of his head. "And that's for runnin' off without even tellin' me where you were goin'."

Stunned by the unexpected punishment, Tannus glanced back at

Delaniya, who merely stared down at him and said, "If you ask me, you just got off easy."

"Hey, at least you didn't get spanked," Dustane said with a smirk, leaving Tannus blushing with embarrassment.

"So, let me make sure I've got this straight," Gram began before leading everyone inside and taking a seat at her kitchen table. "In the middle of a blizzard, you thought it was actually a good idea to follow a spirit all the way out to the Ildarwood. Then you ran away from poor old Etta, got attacked by Cynders, spent a night in the old mines, and *then* decided it might be fun to start a fight between the Asterguards and Cynders, all before almost gettin' yourself killed at High Falls. Now, did I happen to miss anythin' in there, or is that about the gist of it?"

Tannus and Dustane exchanged quick yet anxious looks. "Yeah, that's pretty much it," Tannus mumbled, too ashamed to meet her gaze.

"Well, you're either one of the most foolish boys I've ever met or one of the bravest, and I'm not really sure which," Gram replied. "Do you have any idea what could've happened to you? You could've been killed or Broken, and you're pretty darn lucky you weren't."

"It was all my fault," Dustane confessed, hoping to draw at least some of the blame onto himself. "None of this would've happened if it wasn't for me."

"Oh, really? And who are you?" the old woman demanded.

"I … um … my name is Dustane. Dustane Dulane. My mom and dad live only a few miles up the road, not far from town."

Tannus watched as his gram stared suspiciously at Dustane before rising from her chair and hobbling over to more closely inspect the young boy.

"Dustane, eh?" the old woman asked, her eyes studying Dustane's face as her thin, chapped lips began to smack and pucker. Mere feet away, Tannus froze as he awaited whatever caustic comment she might make next.

"Well, you seem like a nice enough boy," she said finally, causing

Tannus, Dustane, and even Delaniya Brent herself to exhale all at once. "But if my grandson's gonna be friends with you, I'm gonna need you to be a much better influence on him from now on. No more runnin' away into the Ildarwood. No more gettin' into trouble. And for the Heavens' sake, no more startin' fights with Asterguards, Cynders, spirits, or anythin' else that might get you two killed or Broken. You hear me?"

"Yes, ma'am," Tannus and Dustane replied at once.

"Good. Now, what's gonna happen to *him*?" Gram asked the Principal Preceptor, one crooked finger pointing directly at Dustane.

"I'll need to have a word with his parents," said Delaniya. "Several words, in fact. And there's a chance we may need to find him someplace to live that's a bit more … hospitable if that conversation doesn't go well."

Tannus watched as his grandmother nodded, though he could not immediately tell if she fully understood Delaniya's meaning.

"Well, if he needs a place to stay, he's more than welcome to come live here," Gram said with a shrug, catching Tannus and Dustane both by surprise. "We don't have much room, but I can always sleep on the couch so the boys can have their own beds."

Stunned by the offer, Tannus glanced at Dustane, then stepped forward and said, "That's really, really nice, but … didn't you say you can barely afford to take care of me? Never mind two of us."

"We'd find some way to make it work, Tannus," his gram replied. "No one should ever have to live where they're not wanted."

Tannus fell silent, moved beyond words by his gram's unexpected kindness. Yet it was the glimmer of immeasurable gratitude in Dustane's eyes that truly touched Tannus the most.

"That would be most appreciated," said Delaniya, who appeared visibly uncomfortable with all the emotions in the room. "I shall let you know if such generosity will be needed. Now, if there's nothing else, we really must be going."

Suddenly saddened by Dustane's impending departure, Tannus

turned to face him one last time. "You sure you don't want me to come with you?"

"Yeah, I think I'll be all right," Dustane replied, despite how much he feared seeing his parents again. "Thank you for everythin', though, really."

Tannus smiled widely. "You know where to find me if you ever want to hang out again."

"I'll be back before you know it," Dustane cheerfully replied. He could never put into words how much that simple moment meant to him, especially after everything they had both endured.

A GENTLE SNOW fell upon the quiet town of Ranewood that morning, though only a few gray clouds dared wander across the otherwise clear blue skies.

Letting out a sigh as the Principal Preceptor's carriage pulled into the long cobblestone carriageway of the Dulane family home, Dustane could practically sense his parents' resentment the very instant he passed through the invisible barrier around the house.

"It's not too late to change your mind," said Delaniya, seemingly sensing Dustane's thoughts. "We can always find you another home."

"No," he said firmly. "I need to know what they're gonna say, whatever it ends up bein'."

Delaniya nodded understandingly before reaching into her pocket to retrieve a small card. With the Brent family emblem emblazoned upon one side in a sparkling Ildarglass ink, it bore the words *Mrs. Delaniya Brent, Principal Preceptor of Trials, Ranewood* in an elegant font upon the back.

"This is my personal calling card," she said, handing it over. "If you ever need anything, please don't hesitate to use it."

Dustane stared down at the gift and smiled. "Hopefully, I won't need to."

Then together they emerged from the carriage before finally climbing the few Ildarstone steps up to the home's front door. This time around, however, Delaniya knocked with far more authority than she had at Gram's cottage only an hour before.

A few moments later, both of Dustane's parents opened the door.

"Oh no," his mother gasped before bursting into tears and running back inside the house, leaving only his disappointed father to invite them in.

"You'll have to forgive my wife," Mr. Dulane told the Principal Preceptor. "She's still in mourning over Dasia."

"Yes, well … I imagine it'll be much harder to ignore her now that she's gone," Delaniya sternly replied, eliciting an irritated glare from Mr. Dulane.

"You have no idea what it's like to lose a child," he said bitterly. "Let alone two."

"No, thankfully, I do not," said Delaniya. "And were the circumstances different, I might even have more sympathy. But you and I both know this was not some simple case of misidentification at birth, so the child you both claim to have lost never even existed at all."

"She was real to us," Mr. Dulane said, leaving Dustane heartbroken beyond words beside the dour Principal Preceptor.

"Then grieve in private, if you must, and process whatever difficult emotions these past few days have stirred. But right here and now, I need you both to make a choice. Will you commit to loving your own child from this day forward? Or will you step aside and let him be loved by someone who genuinely cares about his happiness?"

Mr. Dulane's mouth fell open, but no words managed to escape for several moments. "I need to speak with my wife for a few minutes, if you'll excuse me."

"Take all the time you need," Delaniya replied as Dustane desperately held back tears.

"I knew they wouldn't want me," he whispered.

So Delaniya knelt beside him and stared directly into his eyes. "Look at me," she insisted, both hands grabbing ahold of Dustane's arm. "No matter what happens here, you are wanted, and you are loved. If not by them, then by people now and in the future who can see you for who you really are and treat you exactly the way that you deserve. But first, we need to give your parents a chance to accept that the family and future they thought they had are gone. And as soon as they do, we will see once and for all what kind of people they truly are. But regardless of how they react, you must know for certain that what they do and say next is in no way whatsoever a reflection on your worth."

Finding strength in the Principal Preceptor's firm grip and reassuring words, Dustane reluctantly nodded. Then he watched with bated breath as his mother and father begrudgingly returned to the central hall.

"Well?" Delaniya asked abruptly.

Dustane's mother and father glanced at each other, both still refusing to gaze into the eyes of their frightened son.

"We lost our firstborn son last winter," Mr. Dulane explained, even as his wife held back tears beside him. "It was … the absolute worst day of our lives, and we've blamed Dasia for it ever since."

"The daughter you called Dasia was never real," Delaniya insisted. "So as far as you or anyone else is concerned, that name is dead, and according to well-established traditions, it should *never* be used again. But the child standing here before you is very much alive, and *his* name is Dustane Dulane. He may not look or sound or even act like the child you knew, but he is real, he is hurting, and he regrets what happened with Demitris every bit as much as you do, if not more. All he's asking for from the two of you is the chance to help each other heal and move on together. Now, is *that* really too much of a burden for you both to bear?"

Mr. and Mrs. Dulane exchanged glances once more before Mr. Dulane finally stared down in the direction of Dustane. "We'll need to change some things in your room and get you all new clothes," he offered, even as Mrs. Dulane began to cry. "Why don't you head on upstairs, and we'll be up to check on you in a little bit?"

Dustane could hardly believe his ears. Staring up at Delaniya Brent one last time, he awaited her nod of approval before promptly running up the stairs.

He had barely set foot in his old room before a sudden idea crossed his mind. Pretending to close the door behind him, he waited patiently for his parents and Delaniya to resume their conversation.

"I sincerely hope you will *both* make an honest effort to care for that sweet boy from now on," Delaniya said firmly, "if not because it is the *right* thing to do, then because of this. If I hear so much as a whisper that you are abusing or neglecting him in any way, I will be back, and I will bring every Asterguard in town with me. And right before they bind you with chains and cart you away to the Lands Beyond Our Lands, I sincerely hope you will both stop and appreciate the irony that, in the end, it was *you* who ended up locked away, never to be seen or heard from again."

Then Dustane watched as the Principal Preceptor took one menacing step toward his parents. "Now, am I understood?" she asked quietly, making each and every last syllable linger on her lips to ensure her point was clearly made.

"Yes," the two parents answered bitterly.

"Good."

Dustane breathed a sigh of relief as he closed the door to his room at last. He could hardly believe how utterly miserable he had been only a few days before, let alone how very much had changed since then.

Yet as he stared at all the florid purple decor around him, he shook his head and wondered how long it would be before his parents actually took the time to redecorate his room.

Trying to imagine how much better everything would look in shades of cerulean blue, he allowed himself a fleeting smile. "Maybe one day soon this will actually feel like home," he whispered before absent-mindedly running his fingers along the wall.

The next thing he knew, every Ildarwood panel that he touched began to change from purple to blue. Then so too did the three other walls around him. Then the frame of his bed, and each of his pillows and sheets. And last of all was the decorative rug on the floor.

Stunned by what he was seeing, he began to wonder if he had somehow fallen into a dream. But a simple pinch on the arm left him convinced that the house itself had wanted to help him feel at home.

Relieved beyond measure, he walked over to the full-length mirror in the corner of his room and smiled at his reflection. After a short lifetime of heartbreaking struggles and seemingly impossible hopes and dreams, Dustane had finally been reborn.

Epilogue

THE LAST LINGERING remnants of winter in Ranewood had finally begun to fade, just in time for the coming start of spring. In only one week's time, families from all across town would converge on the palatial Astercourt, which stood proudly at the Ildarwood's edge. And from there, they would send every child of age out into the ancient forest to begin their first year of Trials.

Not far from the center of town, Dustane emerged from his room with boundless excitement. After racing down the lone spiral staircase in his family's cavernous front hall, he rushed past their modest Ildarwood tree, then ran directly into the kitchen.

"Breakfast is on the table for you," Mrs. Dulane said without turning around.

Though it was far from the warm and loving welcome Dustane had hoped for, he at least took some comfort in knowing that his parents still acknowledged his presence. And little by little, he was determined to win them over.

After sitting down to eat, he watched the kitchen door intently. At any minute, his family's hired helper, Marsella, would return, her bags overflowing with fresh groceries for the week ahead. And the arrival of fresh groceries almost always meant that everything left over from the week before would be thrown out—including all sorts of food from the icebox that was not anywhere close to spoiled.

Dustane leaped out of his chair with glee the moment Marsella finally arrived. Eager to help her unpack, he brought the first of her bags over to the icebox and promptly began replacing as much as he could.

"You still don't care if I donate all the stuff that's still good, right?" he asked his mother, who could not have been any less interested in such things.

"Do whatever you want with it," she replied. She had never been particularly fond of the unusual taste foods often acquired after lingering in the presence of old snow and fresh Frostwater for too long.

Dustane did not need long to unpack everything Marsella had purchased, and before he knew it, four large bags were overflowing with remnant food from the week before.

"Thank you for doin' all the shoppin' for us," Dustane told Marsella, who merely stared at him and blinked. He had always heard that most Broken rarely ever spoke, but after learning that Etta had somehow recovered from the very same affliction, Dustane held out hope that Marsella might one day find enough strength to repair her own shattered soul too.

Freshly encumbered by the four full bags, Dustane stumbled out through the door and began his miles-long journey along the quiet roads of Ranewood. And in light of the warm, springlike weather, he was determined to reach his dear friend's cottage before any of his more precious parcels fully thawed out.

Dustane arrived over an hour later, though only after stopping more than a few times for short breaks. He always enjoyed the look of astonishment he got from Tannus whenever the golden-haired boy first glimpsed Dustane's bounteous gifts.

"Is that all for us?" Tannus asked before grabbing two of the bags and immediately inspecting their contents. "Hey, Gram! This time he brought bacon!"

"Oh, thank the Heavens for that boy!" she shouted from the other room.

It always brought Dustane so much joy to help his friends.

My friends, he reminded himself each and every time the words crossed his mind.

"What are you two gonna get up to today?" asked Gram. "Not goin' anywhere near the Ildarwood again, I hope."

"No, of course not," Tannus replied as he eagerly restocked their empty icebox.

"You know, you two really shouldn't lie to an old lady," Gram chided. "I haven't completely lost my senses. Now, just promise me yas won't get into any trouble while you're in there."

"Don't worry. I'll make sure he behaves," Dustane replied, drawing a sideways glance from Tannus.

"How are things goin' back home?" Gram asked before sitting down at the kitchen table. "Your mom and dad treatin' you okay?"

Dustane shrugged and took a seat across from her while Tannus continued to unpack. "I think they're doin' the best they can," he reluctantly confessed. "They just bought me some more new clothes, but my mom still barely looks at me, even when we're tryin' to talk. And my dad sometimes asks about my day, so ... I guess that's better than nothin'."

"They might just need more time," Gram replied, even though Dustane could tell she was not entirely convinced of her own hopeful words. "But if anythin' ever changes, and you don't wanna live there any more, you better make sure you let us know. You hear me? I don't care how much food you're able to bring us each week. It's just not worth it if you're not happy."

"I promise, I'll make sure you know," Dustane replied, afraid to even imagine things going back to the way they had been mere months before.

"Okay, everythin' is put away," Tannus announced with a sigh of relief. "You know, I really don't mind goin' all the way to your place from now on. It's really not fair for you to carry this much stuff all by yourself."

"That's okay," said Dustane, never one to inconvenience anyone else. "I can usually manage just fine. But the next time my mom and dad get one of those big bison roasts and forget to have Marsella cook it, I'll make sure to let you know."

"Are you kiddin'?" Gram eagerly replied. "For the Heavens' sake, *I'd* hobble all the way out to your place just to carry one of *those* back. I mean, my goodness. I can't even remember the last time I got to eat a nice roast."

"Just try not to burn it," Tannus teased. "I swear, everythin' she makes always gets overcooked."

"Yeah, well, if there's anyone in this house who can teach me how *not* to burn somethin', it's you," Gram promptly replied, causing Dustane to burst into laughter.

He could always count on Tannus and his gram to brighten his day.

A BEAUTIFUL AFTERNOON awaited Dustane and Tannus that day as they made the short walk up from the cottage to the Ildarwood's closest edge. Sneaking into the woods through a narrow gap in the barrier fence, they felt immediate relief the instant they set foot inside the ancient forest once again. Neither one enjoyed the peculiar feeling of emptiness they increasingly felt with each passing day when they could not return.

"Is this the place you were tellin' me about?" Tannus asked upon reaching the peak of a high, rocky ledge, which looked out over a long-abandoned farm near the center of town.

"Yep. I came out here a few days before Ansolas, right after I heard a couple people in the market whisperin' about their last visit. They said it's called Wisher's Well."

After hiking up one last hill, the two found themselves gazing at last upon the fabled location. Composed entirely of rounded river stones and simple mortar, the well appeared to be hundreds of years old, as did the Ildarwood tree that grew directly beside it. With sparkling crystalline bark, as well as tiny glowing bumps along its gnarled trunk and sprawling branches, the enormous Ildarwood tree had equally massive roots, which had nearly consumed the companion well entirely.

"What do you think's down there?" Tannus asked as he peered into the well's seemingly infinite depths.

"Probably just water and a whole lot of Silver coins, if I had to guess," Dustane replied.

"And you really think your wish is the reason why that spirit went to find you?"

"I mean ... I don't know how else it would've known anythin' about me."

"So what'd you wish for?" asked Tannus, even though he knew Dustane might not answer.

"Somethin' I'm really glad didn't come true," Dustane reluctantly replied. "Somethin' I could never have taken back if it actually had."

Tannus looked away, ashamed of himself for even asking something so personal. Yet only once he was staring off into the forest did he suddenly spot a face he had never expected to see again.

"What? What's wrong?" Dustane asked, surprised that his friend had gone pale.

"I swear I just saw Fynn," Tannus replied. "It was only for a second, but it looked just like him."

"I thought you said he turned into a wisp the last time you saw him."

"He did … at least, I thought he did. But maybe he's slowly startin' to come back. I mean, my gram did say spirits tend to get stronger the more you think about 'em, and I think about Fynn almost all the time."

"Well, maybe he just wanted to see if you're doin' okay," Dustane offered, placing his hand on Tannus's shoulder.

"Either that, or he's tryin' to lead us somewhere else," Tannus said with a momentary smirk, causing Dustane to chuckle at what he first considered to be a joke. But then the two fell silent as they glanced in each other's direction.

Neither needed to speak a word before they both began sprinting into the woods.

"Can you still see him?" Dustane asked between breaths as he struggled to keep up with Tannus.

"Yeah, I think so. It looks like he's just up ahead."

Vigor rushed through their veins as they chased the elusive spirit through the woods, and they did not stop running until they arrived at last beside a long-abandoned settlement in the highest hills of Miner's Reach.

A perimeter of signs barred passage into the ruins, and Tannus and Dustane both recognized what they were each made of at once.

"Wardingwood," they grumbled, the type of Ildarwood always used to keep people out of places where they did not belong. On more than one occasion, the two had crossed paths with the frustrating material, which possessed the unique ability to repulse any souls that moved too close.

"'Do not enter. Unstable grounds ahead. Severe risk of death to all trespassers,'" Dustane read with disappointment. "Well, I'm pretty sure this is *exactly* the kind of place your gram wanted me to keep you out of, so maybe we should just head back."

"Are you kiddin'?" asked Tannus. "Now I wanna go inside even more."

Dustane winced before staring suspiciously at his friend. "You know, I'm beginnin' to think your gram was right. Maybe you really *are* a bad influence on me."

Tannus laughed and shrugged, with no small measure of pride in his smile. "Look, do you wanna go see what Fynn was tryin' to lead us to or not?"

"Argh. Okay, fine," Dustane conceded. "Do you wanna do it this time, or should I?"

"Why don't we both do it?" Tannus answered.

Aiming one hand each in the direction of the two nearest signs, Dustane and Tannus focused all their attention on summoning some of the raw spectral energy flowing deep within their souls. Neither one wanted to fail in front of the other.

Two bright flashes lit up the woods that afternoon, and within seconds, both signs crumbled into a fine black dust—one consumed entirely by Goldenfire flames, while the other succumbed to the soul-sapping cold of a direct Frostwater blast.

"After you," Tannus said politely, leaving Dustane to shake his head and shove Tannus forward.

"Yeah, nice try. If anyone's gonna walk in there first, it's you."

Proceeding into the abandoned settlement with utmost caution, Dustane and Tannus marveled at the destruction and decay all around them. What had most certainly once been a beautiful village had become overgrown by both Ildarwood and greenwood trees, with untold generations of untamed weeds and briars wherever they looked. Enormous craters had formed in and around the main square—the clear result of caved-in mines—and almost every house they could see stood precariously on the verge of collapse after decades of neglect.

"Hey, look over there," said Tannus, drawing Dustane's attention toward two short pillars—both apparently once broken before being mended by hands unknown. Placed atop each one was a small box made of Ildarwood—the first with a glowing amber stone in the center of its lid, and the second with a pale sapphire crystal.

"Who do you think left these here?" Dustane asked suspiciously, his eyes searching the surrounding town for any subtle signs of another person.

"I'm guessin' someone who knew we'd come all the way here and find 'em," Tannus replied.

Opening his box first, Tannus was surprised to find a tarnished piece of Silverwood waiting within. Carefully carved into the hilt of a sword, it had the words *Forged by Fire* delicately etched on one side. And directly underneath it, Tannus discovered a small envelope with a simple card inside.

"What does it say?" Dustane asked eagerly.

"'When all is lost and hope is gone, we light the night until the dawn,'" Tannus recited. "What do you think it means?"

"I have no idea," Dustane replied before carefully opening the box with the sapphire stone. Within he found a similar hilt, only this one had the words *Endure Any Winter* carefully etched into it.

"What are you two doing out here?" a stern voice demanded, nearly causing Tannus and Dustane both to leap out of their skin.

Promptly hiding the gifts behind their backs, they stared at the old woman, who stood impatiently upon the other side of the abandoned square. Dressed in a dated gray dress and matching cloak, she walked with a tarnished cane made of Silverwood, and she wore a bitter expression upon her face.

"We thought we saw our friend come out here, so we were just tryin' to find him," Tannus honestly replied, earning a suspicious stare from the old woman. "Any chance you've seen him?"

"I have not seen anyone out here in years," the old woman replied, her accent so distinctly formal that it reminded Dustane at once of the pompous planner his parents had hired to prepare their housewarming back in Amberdale. And according to Mrs. Dulane at the time, only people from the Avylaan Kingdom ever spoke in such a manner.

"Then I guess we'll just be goin'," said Tannus, deathly afraid of the woman's penetrating stare.

"Before we go," Dustane chimed in suddenly, catching Tannus and the woman both by surprise, "do you happen to know what happened to this place?"

The old woman glanced at the crumbling structures around her. "Most of this was the Astyrians' doing," she bitterly replied. "This village used to house all the children they sent down into the mines. And that building right there was where they all went to school."

Pointing toward the charred schoolhouse high upon a cliff at the edge of the village, she said, "My husband used to teach there, right up until the day he died."

"Did he die in the fire?" Tannus dared inquire. The question alone was enough to cause momentary flashes from his past to briefly haunt him.

"Regrettably, yes, almost twenty years ago. He was a good and honest man, and he deserved a far more honorable end. Now, you two really must be going. This place has seen far too much suffering over the years, and there are more than a few spirits in this part of the woods who are particularly dangerous, so you would both do well to avoid them."

"It's a little bit late for that," Tannus whispered, earning a sudden elbow from Dustane.

"If it's so dangerous to come out here, then why do you still visit?" Dustane asked the old woman, genuinely concerned for her safety.

"For one thing, someone has to try and keep the memory of my late husband alive," she said somberly. "And unlike the two of you, no one would ever miss *me* if I was gone."

Saddened by the old woman's words, Dustane took a few steps

forward. "You know, I used to think that about myself too. But then I came out here, and the Ildarwood helped me find new friends, like him. So maybe one day, somethin' like that will happen for you too, as long as you don't give up hope."

The old woman's eyes narrowed as she considered Dustane's words. "I am far too old to make new friends," she said with disappointment, "and the very last remnants of my hope died with my husband. Now, if you will both please excuse me, I would very much like to grieve in peace."

Heartbroken by the old woman's story, Dustane nodded respectfully before walking with Tannus back into the outer woods.

"Well, that was really creepy," said Tannus, "but at least we got these first."

"Yeah," Dustane mumbled, still secretly wishing that he could somehow help the mourning stranger.

"So, did yours have a note too?" asked Tannus, causing Dustane to stop suddenly in his tracks.

"Oh, um … I forgot to look." And upon opening the box once more, he found a small envelope waiting beneath the Silverwood handle inside. Caught off guard by its unexpected weight, Dustane opened it carefully before emptying the first of its contents into his hand.

"What is *that*?" Tannus asked with surprise, having never before seen an Ildarglass coin with a pale blue glow.

Dustane fell silent, his face far more pallid than usual. "I think it's the coin I dropped in Wisher's Well … the one I whispered my wish into the day before that awful spirit came to find me."

Tannus's mouth fell open. "What about the card? What does it say?" he asked with bated breath.

Dustane's fingers began to tremble as he fumbled with the small handwritten card.

"Well?" asked Tannus, his gaze fixed upon the back of the mysterious note.

Dustane met his stare before finally turning the card in his direction.

A lesson learned, lest you forget.
Don't wish for things you might regret.

THE END

Afterword

I created the world of the Ildarwood as a magical escape for readers of almost any age and background, for far too many have experienced challenging trials of their own—especially while they were still quite young. To me, there are few things more heartbreaking than when innocent children are forced to endure the harsh realities of life before they've even had a chance to experience a full and normal childhood.

That is why the Ildarwood exists. To give readers a chance to get away from whatever struggles they may be dealing with every day, even if only for a few minutes at a time. To give imaginative children a magical world to call their own—a place where they can unlock their hidden gifts and discover the most incredible versions of themselves. And to give adults the opportunity to relive their childhoods in an ancient forest where things just might have turned out differently.

But the story of Dustane Dulane is especially important, because it provides a unique perspective most readers will never get to see—that of a child who was born with a heart and mind inherently at odds with their physical self. Too few people truly understand the trauma endured by children who are born different through no fault of their own. That is in part why these children experience homelessness, self-harm, and suicide at alarmingly high rates—often before they're even old enough to drive.

The portrayal of Dustane's life in this book is a simple allegory—though one that has been carefully and lovingly crafted to help readers understand the struggle of similar children through the lens of a fantasy world. But real children like Dustane often know from an early age that the person they are inside doesn't match their body or their given name. And quite tragically, they are often forced to make a terrible choice—spend every single day pretending to be someone they're not, or risk immediate and severe harm from family and strangers alike.

That is why it was so important to me that a story like Dustane's be told, and why I will forever donate all proceeds from the sale of this book to charities for high-risk homeless youth. It may not be much, but every dollar raised and every mind changed can make a huge difference for some innocent child.

So if you enjoyed reading this book, please consider sharing it with other readers who might benefit from its lessons.

It might just save a life.

S. C. Selvyn

Lore of the Ildarwood

A Collection of Short Stories

The Legend of Arcus

T HERE ARE FEW Ildarwood trees left in the world that still remember the ancient times, though one in particular stands within the hallowed halls of a sacred court. For three thousand years at least, it has preserved the memories of those heroic souls who dared fight back against a brutal conqueror. Yet few amongst those honored names are quite so revered as that of a simple man who one day went on to become a legend.

His life began like most, born to a family of common farmers with neither names nor deeds of note. Near the sole Ildarian forest on Dia— but one of a thousand islands within the Nine Denycian Seas—Arcus was raised by hardworking parents. Like them and each of his eight older siblings, he toiled day and night, never one to cause trouble or complain.

On the first day of spring after his twelfth birthday, he began his Trials like countless children before him. Entering the Ildarian woodlands with others his age, he had no reason to believe his Trials would be any different from their own. Yet as they each came to master their elemental gifts, one by one, Arcus found himself unable to perform such a feat.

Using cunning and stealth to survive instead, Arcus relied upon his skill with farming to provide food for his pack. Then through his mastery of an Ildarian bow, he quickly learned to contribute to their shared defense.

Four long years did Arcus spend in the Ildarwood before his Trials came to an end. He had no way of knowing how much had changed outside the forest while he had been gone.

Ash and embers were all that remained of his family farm by the time he had reached it, and none but his eldest sister still survived to recount what had transpired. During the previous year, a new Imperial Anax had been crowned in Ethynia, the Denycian capital. Known as Xanthilis, the Golden Fist of the Namosian Sea, he had risen to power after launching a brutal campaign across dozens of islands in the region, gathering soldiers and supplies for his vast naval fleets along the way. And all who opposed his efforts were forced to watch as everyone and everything they loved was ruthlessly consumed by spectral fire.

Nearly left Broken by the discovery, Arcus sought out each of his companions from his time in the sacred woods, but none among them dared rise up against the Golden Fist. And even when he turned to his sister, he found her so very close to becoming Broken herself that nothing he said could compel her to fight in the name of revenge.

In the days that followed, Arcus traveled from village to village around the island in search of those with kindred spirits. But before he could even amass enough crew to sail a ship of modest size, the Eyes of Xanthilis had already reported the activities of Arcus to the nearest loyal vessel.

A detachment of five soldiers was sent to punish him, and they arrived at night to avoid any chance of warning. So many times before had they silenced the enemies of Xanthilis in their sleep that they had no reason to doubt their mission would succeed. But when they arrived in the village where the farm of Arcus and his family had once stood, what they found instead was a silent shadow, quick and nimble, which moved through the town unseen. Armed with Ildarglass arrows, Arcus hunted down all five assassins. And in one final act of cunning, he used their ship to make a daring escape.

From island to island across the Nine Denycian Seas, Arcus traveled for months, his desperate search for new companions almost entirely in vain. Only a handful of men was he able to recruit to his side, for the Eyes of Xanthilis were plentiful, and the bounty on his head seemed to grow by the day.

Three years into his search, and running low on options, Arcus decided to try his luck in the furthest reaches of the ninth Denycian sea—a treacherous region referred to by most as the Cursed Isles. Arcus had barely even entered the outer reaches of their uncharted waters when a terrible storm arose as if from nowhere and promptly destroyed his precious ship, leaving him and his entire crew stranded upon the nearest island.

Known as an inhospitable rock where even the most battle-hardened sailors would be devoured alive by the natives, the isle of Galea had long been feared by any captain worth their salt. Yet much to the surprise of Arcus, what he found upon the island instead was thousands of civilized people who lived in colorful villages throughout the forests.

Welcomed along with his crew, Arcus was treated like a god by the men who had discovered him lying on the shore. He was pampered with elaborate meals and warm baths for days on end. And by the end of his first week, he very nearly considered abandoning his quest for good. But when brutal nightmares about the fate of his family forced him awake night after night, he knew with utmost certainty that he would never find true peace so long as Xanthilis and his kind still ruled.

By all accounts, Arcus requested an audience with the island elders on the morning of his eighth day of rest. Yet only after consulting with them was he allowed to meet with the one true ruler of Galea. Nearly seven feet tall, with flawless brown skin and a body so exquisitely proportioned that few women could ever compete, she had silver-white hair that flowed up toward the Heavens like a river of silk before cascading gently down one side of her flawless face. And her iridescent gown reflected every color known to man and more, with countless gemstones delicately woven into the fabric to resemble shimmering stars in a midnight sky.

But by far the most mesmerizing feature that Arcus beheld that day was the woman's bright, prismatic eyes, which made her stares so incredibly penetrating that Arcus was entirely convinced she could gaze directly through his soul.

"You stand before the Living Goddess Herself, Essencia—Our Lady of Divine Opulence and Queen of All Queens, Her Majesty, the High and Most Exalted Mother of Dragos, and Sacred Sovereign of All Secrets across the Nine Denycian Seas."

Everyone in the court knelt as she savored every tantalizing moment of their worship. Flanked by her most devoted attendants, she pursed her lips and inspected each guest from afar before finally turning her attention back to Arcus.

"Come," she beckoned at long last, compelling her guest to approach her lavish throne by way of an elaborate walkway in the center of the court.

"The Golden Fist of the Namosian Sea is coming," said Arcus, "and none so far have been able to stand against him. Countless families have been lost to his brutality, including my own, and I fear what might happen to your warm and welcoming people should he ever decide to claim your paradise shores."

"If you have only come to warn us, Arcus of Dia, then you have made your journey in vain, for the Eyes of Xanthilis are no match for the Gaze of Galea. Our eyes and ears extend far beyond the Nine Denycian Seas, and our agents risk their lives every day to ensure the Golden Fist will never come."

"I have not merely brought words of warning," said Arcus. "I also stand before you, great goddess of Galea, in the Wise and Ancient House of Essencia, and I beg of you … please, grant me whatever men or aid you can spare, and help me topple this merciless conqueror before any more harm can be done. Your people may be safe for now, but countless others are not, and I fear that once all others have fallen, Xanthilis and his men will have no one left to conquer but you."

Stirred by the impassioned pleas, the goddess Essencia consulted briefly with her attendants before turning her prismatic gaze back to Arcus once more. "We are not a warlike people. We have few weapons and ships to offer. Only shelter and food, secrets and counsel. Take as much of each as you wish, plus one small ship, should you still choose to pursue your noble cause. Or you may choose to remain here with your crew and enjoy paradise for however long you wish to stay."

"How long do you expect paradise to remain if you and your people refuse to take up arms in your own defense?" Arcus challenged.

"Our people do not fight," proclaimed Essencia. "For a thousand years or more, very few without our welcome have successfully set foot upon our shores. And in all that time, we have yet to face a storm we could not weather on our own."

"You have *never* faced a storm like this," said Arcus. "I beg of you, please at least grant me permission to seek out aid from the other islands and nations around this sea. Let me *try* to form an alliance and rally enough able souls to form a viable shield against the Golden Fist. It will cost you nothing except your word to join, should the alliance one day acquire sufficient strength."

Silence fell upon the House of Essencia, though whispers amongst her attendants quickly followed. But Essencia showed no desire to consult with them this time around. The decision was hers, and hers alone.

"We will give you a map to all the other islands nearby. You may visit each with my blessing," said Essencia. "And should the day you speak of ever come, then I will rally whatever forces I can in shared defense."

It was the first true victory for Arcus, but it would not be his last.

From the shores of Galea, Arcus took what few remaining crewmen he could convince to sail from paradise, and one by one, he visited every inhabited island near Galea.

On the isle of Dragos—the original home of Essencia herself—Arcus spoke with families from a dozen Sacred Houses, nearly all of them ruled by a proud and oath-sworn Mother. From them, he was promised the greatest spies, assassins, and shade throwers they had to offer, should a viable alliance ever be forged.

Next came the volcanic isle of Oneiros, where violent eruptions were so cataclysmically common that seafaring vessels often steered well clear of the island's crimson skies and plumes of ash. Forced to navigate through sandy shoals whilst in the throes of treacherous tides, Arcus and his crew barely survived the perilous journey. But when they arrived at last on the coral-colored shore, they were greeted not by flaming skies and molten rock.

Far to the contrary, the isle was more like paradise than it appeared from afar. Perpetually shielded from the outside world by an elaborate illusion of spectral wind, Oneiros was covered by a seemingly endless sea of Ildarian trees and ruby leaves. Even the mountain's volcanic peak appeared restful, despite the thick black clouds of smoke and ash that rose up from its center now and again.

All across the island, settlers from various cultures lived in harmony, and the leaders among them were as diverse as any could possibly be. Yet one thing did every person have in common, Arcus noticed, and that was their unabashed use of Crimsonwind to carefully alter their appearance, each with reasons all their own.

The council they called was unanimous in their ruling. They had few weapons, shields, and soldiers they could offer, but should the need ever arise, they would send their greatest illusionists to aid in shared defense. And so, Arcus continued on to the next of the Cursed Isles.

Anderis was as peculiar an island as Arcus had ever seen. From the sea, it appeared completely unremarkable, little more than rocks and trees barely even peeking above the sea. But once Arcus made his way to the island's center, he found villages entirely unalike each other in almost every regard. Some were filled with perfectly common people whose only true distinction was that they were neither men nor women called, while other settlements had villagers who were as wild and eccentric as the most exotic of tropical birds.

Their leaders again offered little in the way of military support, but amongst their numbers were some with a particularly valuable gift—the elusive craft of "indistinction." With unique souls that could render them unnoticed in a crowd, they would be able to move without detection, should they ever be called for such a purpose.

Yet amongst all the inhabitants of Anderis, it was the people of Oranios Village alone, with their fluorescent clothes and wild hair, who volunteered for any covert missions involving fomented rebellions or sabotage. Banished from their native lands for their defiant nature and unusual appearances, they were especially eager to cause chaos in the streets of any city where cruelty and violence were used to repress the helpless masses.

Last of all, Arcus visited the distant isle of Labyris, where he and his crew encountered forces unlike any they had ever experienced before. The first was a massive flock of ravishing women, who wore distractingly scant attire. Soaring overhead with the aid of enormous Ildarglass wings, they sang songs so incredibly hypnotic that the entire crew swiftly succumbed to unbridled fits of convulsive ecstasy. Arcus alone stood immune to their seductions.

After guiding the ship safely to shore all by himself, Arcus was next met by a ferocious guard of powerful women. Wearing Ildarglass armor and horned helms, they resembled great taurine beasts, and the strongest amongst them were armed with menacing double-bladed axes called labryses. Far from hospitable to outsiders, the Labyrisians and their leaders ridiculed Arcus for even suggesting the need for an alliance, for none had ever defeated the island's soldiers in battle.

"You come and speak of threats from a distant land," said one of the oldest Labyrisians brought to court, "but what great armies have you rallied to your cause? The Galeans would rather spend their days tending to their flowers or their fruits than carrying a banner off to war. And the kings and queens of Dragos know far more about pageantry than fighting. The thinly veiled faces of Oneiros would rather run and hide in their hills than wield a sword. And the island of Anderis has naught but useless philosophers and meddlesome rogues amongst their ranks. What good would any of them do in the forge of battle?"

Nothing Arcus said thereafter was enough to convince the Labyrisian leaders, but before he left their court for good, he dared to impart one final thought: "When the Galeans fall, there will be no fruits or flowers to decorate your halls. And when the kings and queens of Dragos are slain, there will be no one leading the parades to celebrate your victories. When the thinly veiled faces of Oneiros are battered and bruised, you will hear no songs of praise when you win a battle. And when the philosophers and rogues of Anderis are silenced, there will be none left to speak out on your behalf when imperial ships invade your shores. You will be entirely alone in your victories, then entirely alone in your grand defeat. But at least you will all go down fighting, knowing that right up until the end, you accomplished even *that* entirely on your own."

Arcus returned to sea that very night, banished with his crew and commanded never to return.

Little sleep came to Arcus during the journey back to Galea, for each and every time he closed his eyes, he saw only the haunting images of all the islands he had visited engulfed entirely in spectral flames.

He arrived back on the shores of Galea just before the rise of a crimson dawn. Bowing his head with shame, he entered the House of Essencia and reported his failure directly to the goddess herself.

"How unfortunate," she told him. "While you were gone, we heard disturbing whispers from Ethynia. It appears you were right. The Golden Fist has indeed set his sights on the Cursed Isles, and within days, he will send a small fleet to claim them as his own. Sadly, he is not expecting any of us to put up much of a fight."

"But you are a goddess," said Arcus. "Can't you conjure another great storm to protect this island, just as you've done so many times before?"

"Such grand illusions only work on small ships with small crews," one of the attendants begrudgingly confessed. "And only a handful among us even know how to conjure them that well."

"Then let me sail back to each island and try to rally their troops at once!" Arcus implored.

"Even if you could," said Essencia, "they would never make it here in time. Not with nearly enough ships or soldiers to make a difference."

Arcus shook his head with disbelief. "What about all your eyes and ears across the Nine Seas and beyond? Surely *they* must be able to help in some way."

"We have many spies and assassins in the streets and great halls of Ethynia," said Essencia, "but none have ever gotten close to Xanthilis. The Golden Fist wears Ildarian armor night and day, and he has at the center of his court the largest Spitewood tree the world has ever seen— one that only grows more powerful as his followers become increasingly fueled by hate. And thanks to the oaths he has forced his soldiers and servants to swear upon that tree, their souls and fates are forever bound to it and him. So should any amongst them so much as think about betraying him, they will immediately burst into Goldenfire flames."

"In short," said another loyal attendant, "it would seem that Xanthilis is, in every possible sense, untouchable."

"Never in the histories of any land has there been a person beyond the reach of *every* weapon," said Arcus. "We just need to figure out which one can fell a man who can never be touched. So tell me, noble goddess of Galea, what great secrets of Xanthilis and his soldiers do you keep? Perhaps there is one we might use to our advantage."

Historians say that Essencia merely raised an eyebrow at first. Then she turned to her attendants and said, "Take him to the library. And serve him as much tea as he can drink."

Days passed as Arcus combed through every secret record the Galeans had made about Xanthilis, his generals, the city of Ethynia, and all the major leaders in and around the capital. All the while, the goddess herself was paying visits to each of the Cursed Isles to respect-fully request their urgent aid. And by the time Arcus and Essencia met again, it was with leaders from Dragos, Oneiros, and Anderis, plus a single highly-skeptical representative from Labyris too.

"I believe I have discovered a possible flaw in the impenetrable armor of Xanthilis," said Arcus. "Amongst his men, a single affliction of the soul has been appearing time and again. It is an incredibly rare form of the Blight, one which causes uncontrollable rage in any spirit bound to the golden flames of Ildaris. And so devastating are the effects that whenever one of his soldiers has become infected in the past, the others have immediately shattered his soul to prevent any further spread. So far, they have had great success in keeping it contained, but I think I know how we can use it to our advantage."

"A contagion of the soul would take weeks or months to spread amongst his forces," said Essencia. "I fear the Golden Fist will fall upon these islands long before any such Blight could take effect."

Arcus then smiled in response and said, "The Golden Fist cannot slam down upon us if he has neither eyes to see nor a head to think. First we must use the Gaze of Galea to blind him. Then we can send a small force to Ethynia to covertly destroy his inner circle."

"And what about the forty-odd Denycian triremes that are already on their way here?" asked the sole representative from Labyris. "That is over eight thousand battle-hardened soldiers. We would need every Lab-yrisian warrior to join the fight. Then, even if we somehow managed to win, we would hardly stand a chance against a larger, retaliatory strike."

"Then we will just need to ensure the second wave will never come," Arcus announced defiantly. "Let us gather whatever forces we can to defend Galea from the first assault. And if each island will provide me with their bravest and finest few, then I shall lead them to Ethynia myself to secure our victory."

It was a plan with little chance of success, though the only one of merit anyone could offer. So with final agreement among them, the leaders returned to their islands to prepare their people for the battle ahead.

The first ships from Oneiros and Anderis arrived within days, each completely filled with volunteers from their shores. Next came dozens of ships from Dragos—two days late but filled to capacity with ferocious fighters and an entire hold full of overflowing trunks.

Yet by the evening when Arcus prepared to set sail from Galea one last time, the only island he had not yet heard from was Labyris—though few among the Galeans were particularly surprised.

"Are you entirely certain you are prepared to take this risk on our behalf?" the goddess Essencia asked as Arcus boarded his ship with the last of his new crew.

"I do this not for you or Galea, or even for myself," said Arcus. "I do this for all the countless children in the world who should never have to fear the golden fires of war. And should my blood be spilled by battle's end, then I shall use it to paint the skies with every color of our banners—a sign for all to see that in the end, our disparate peoples rose together to fight as one."

"Noble sentiments," said Essencia. "But alas, the brave Labyrisians have still refused to join our cause."

"I still have faith," Arcus said with a smile. "When we need them most, I am certain they will rise and fight beside us as our kin."

Setting sail under a crimson sky at dusk, Arcus and his crew remained concealed under the cover of darkness right up until the following dawn. Then he made use of all the skilled illusionists on his crew to sail directly past an entire fleet of Denycian warships—each with its sights set solely on Galea.

Not until just after midnight that next day did Arcus and his brave companions finally pull into the Ethynian harbor. Disguised as nothing more than drunken sailors, they drew little attention from imperial guards as they disembarked from their ship, just a few at a time, every hour till dawn. And once a golden sun did rise over the city, Arcus and the remainder of his followers made use of the bustling city streets to conceal their travels throughout the day.

Back on Galea, it was the Queen of All Queens herself who prepared the united island forces for an imminent attack. With forty sails bearing the Golden Fist's emblem growing larger on the horizon, over one hundred small fishing boats—hardly a match for the Denycian triremes and their crews—slowly traveled out to sea, each with specialized crews for the specific tasks they had been given.

The Denycian fleet had received clear orders: demand a surrender if they could, but make an example if they must. Yet the men in golden armor had heard more than a few rumors about the fabled isle of Galea, and many among them wanted nothing more than to unleash swift and unrepentant brutality upon every inhabitant they could find.

Having approached the shores from all sides, the Denycians sent dozens of rowboats full of soldiers onto the glittering beaches to overwhelm any defenses. The last few smaller vessels had barely begun the trip before flames of every color began burning the sails of all the mother ships, causing panic across the decks. Then bolts of emerald lightning appeared as if from nowhere, causing half a dozen rowboats to explode while the soldiers on board went soaring high into the air.

"Fire at will!" all the captains began to shout. They knew at once that deception was afoot. Noticing subtle mirages all around them, they began to target seemingly empty swaths of the surrounding sea, only to reveal now and again that a Galean boat and its crew had been concealed from view by spectral illusions.

But it was already too late for the Denycians, for by the time the Galean boats had been discovered, ruthless agents from the Dragosian

House of Skiá had already snuck on board the enormous warships. One by one, they threw paralyzing bursts of spectral shade at every archer and flinger of flames who crossed their path.

On the island shores, the invading soldiers began seething with rage. Compelled to slaughter every last Galean they could find as well-deserved punishment for the surprise attacks, they raced toward the nearest villages with their flaming swords drawn and eyes ablaze. They never expected to be met by enormous, muscular men in thick Ildarian armor. With helms carefully crafted to resemble ferocious ursine beasts, the island defenders swung thick brown clubs made of the strongest Fermwood on Galea, sending one invader after another crashing violently into nearby rocks and towering trees. Seemingly immune to spectral flames, the Galean knights laughed as Ildarglass swords and arrows alike shattered harmlessly against them time and again.

The battle, it appeared, had been won, but the Galeans knew the war was far from over. Watching helplessly as Denycian messengers took to the skies with the aid of golden Ildarglass wings, the goddess Essencia warned that Xanthilis would send the rest of his ships to Galea just as soon as word reached him of his initial fleet's defeat. So it was then up to Arcus to sever the Denycian head before its Golden Fist could strike again.

With shrouds of spectral shadows to hide them, Arcus and a handful of his followers made their way discreetly through the darkened alleyways of Ethynia at night. And once they arrived at a seemingly vacant building, which stood just outside the imperial palace walls, they were allowed inside by a lovely maiden with sparkling emerald eyes. From there, they entered a secret passageway in the cellar. Then they ever so carefully made their way into the lowest levels of the palace itself.

Few patrolling guards did they find in the hallways they traveled with the aid of the emerald-eyed girl, though time and again, they passed rooms and corridors with armored men either asleep or taken ill. The Gaze of Galea had successfully cleared the way for a final attack.

Arcus entered the imperial court that night armed with his Ildarian bow and a quiver full of prismatic arrows. At his side stood the best assassins and warriors from across each of the so-called Cursed Isles. All that remained was eliminating Xanthilis himself—the Imperial Anax of Denycia and the Golden Fist of the Namosian Sea.

Flanked by his most trusted defenders, Xanthilis was prepared to defend his reign at any cost. Yet far more impressive to Arcus than either Xanthilis himself or his great gilded throne was the mythic Spitewood tree behind them both. Standing proud and tall in the center of an enormous stone tower, it was exposed on only a single side, while at its feet were positioned a handful of elite Denycian guards—each one utterly determined to keep it safe.

Goldenfire flames soared across the court as flames of every color immediately soared back in the opposite direction. Ildarglass arrows exploded against walls and suits of armor, but those that hit their marks sent invisible shockwaves of raw spectral energy exploding out in all directions. Stormspark bolts and Frostwater streams were met with ferocious spectral fires, neutralizing each other instantly in flight.

Flashes of light lit up the skies around the palace, drawing the attention of soldiers and guards, as well as concerned civilians in the streets.

One by one, the defenders of Arcus and Xanthilis both fell until only the men themselves still remained. Xanthilis was exhausted, but stood ready and armed with a golden sword made of burning Ildarian glass. Across the court, Arcus was down to his final three arrows and hardly a match for someone as experienced in combat as the infamous Golden Fist.

"Go ahead," Xanthilis taunted. "Shoot at will. But even if I die here today, know this. My fleet already has its orders, and by the coming dawn, they will set sail to burn every last one of the Cursed Isles to the ground. Men, women, and children all. Then perhaps the plague that is your people will finally be purged at last."

Infuriated by the cruel savagery of the man standing before him,

Arcus let loose two of his last three arrows. But when Xanthilis expertly evaded them both, Arcus knew he needed to make his final arrow count.

Running at Xanthilis, his last prismatic bolt raised high like a spear, Arcus knew he would not survive the fateful encounter he had dreamed about for years. He just needed to ensure Xanthilis went down with him.

Desperate to avoid the Golden Fist's burning blade, Arcus made every possible effort to drive his final arrow into the emperor's savage heart. But before he could, Xanthilis drove his sword directly into the beating chest of Arcus, forcing him to collapse onto the ground.

"Too bad your other puny arrows missed," Xanthilis whispered, savoring every intoxicating moment of his enemy's suffering.

Yet in his final moments, Arcus smiled up at Xanthilis and said, "They were never meant for you."

Confused by the unexpected last words of his would-be assassin, Xanthilis turned to discover that both of the Ildarglass arrows he had so expertly evaded were firmly embedded in the ever-burning trunk of the enormous Spitewood tree behind the throne. Thinking nothing of them at first, he barely noticed the subtle prismatic glow emanating from both. But ever so slowly, the enormous golden tree became consumed by flames of every color.

"What have you done?" Xanthilis demanded.

"I just needed to find a soldier whose soul had become infected with the Golden Blight," Arcus managed. "Then I dipped all my arrows in a pool of his tainted Silverblood. Now all the rage and blinding fury you have used to amass your power for years ... it's slowly burning into the heart of your precious Spitewood tree, and soon it'll make its way into the souls of every last person who ever pledged their loyalty to you."

Xanthilis could hardly believe what he was hearing. Terrified by the spreading flames of every color, Xanthilis ran to escape, but immediately found himself hobbled by a single masterful strike.

Stumbling over to Xanthilis, Arcus plucked his last prismatic arrow from the fallen emperor's heel. "You were the one who started this fire," said Arcus. "And now you'll *finally* get to experience all the pain and suffering it's caused."

Immeasurable fear compelled Xanthilis to crawl desperately toward the nearest door, while Arcus knelt with exhaustion and readied his bow for one last shot. Holding the tip of his final arrow against his own spectral wound, Arcus stained the Ildarglass with his dying thoughts, then bound its very existence to his soul. And with the last of his strength, he released the arrow out into the night, leaving a fine prismatic mist trailing behind it.

A massive explosion followed as all the hatred stored within the burning Spitewood tree finally erupted into the halls of the imperial court, scorching and shattering every last living soul that it could find. Yet all the while, a sparkling ribbon of every color stretched as far as the eye could see—the final gift of Arcus, and an enduring sign that his promise had been kept.

Back on Galea, the goddess Essencia and her council of leaders watched the horizon for any further signs of Denycian warships. But the great sails of the Golden Fist never appeared.

It was days later before anyone on the island finally learned why.

In the hours leading up to the attack on Galea, the Labyrisians had secretly sent their sirens to every Denycian port and ship that they could find. And once all the captains and crews had finally succumbed to the intoxicating effects of their seductive songs, Labyrisian axe-maidens and enormous women in taurine battle armor had begun unleashing their fury upon every vile man in golden armor that had crossed their path. So by the following dawn, once all was finally said and done, nearly every remote ship in the Denycian fleet had either been destroyed or robbed of its crew.

In less than one week's time, the largest empire in the world had suddenly fallen, and all the people across the Nine Denycian Seas were finally free.

ONE YEAR HAD passed before the first large celebrations were held to honor those lost in the battles to save the Cursed Isles. Taking place on the neutral island of Enomenos, the memorial ceremony was presided over by Essencia herself, though at her side were leaders from Dragos, Oneiros, Anderis, and Labyris.

Atop the great waterfalls of Enomenos, one of the rarest Ildarwood trees ever discovered was planted in the center of a cliffside island. With bark and leaves of every color, it would stand as an eternal symbol of the solidarity of the surrounding islands, which were collectively renamed the Arcus Isles in eternal honor of the fallen hero.

And in the ground where the Ildarian eucalyptus tree grew, Essencia buried the final arrow that Arcus had ever loosed from his bow—discovered by a loyal agent of Galea in one of the city's public gardens. With his memories and soul forever bound to the arrow, they could endure for as long as the Euwood tree continued to keep it safe.

In the centuries that followed, the sacrifice of Arcus would never be forgotten, and his legend would spread to every corner of the world. And whenever a child was born holding a stone of every color, just like Arcus, they were said to have an Arcusian soul.

The Legend of Sahar

I N ANCIENT TIMES, before the dawn of spectral science, there was no way of knowing before birth if a child possessed an unusual soul. And in far too many cases, years or even decades would pass before the true nature of the child was fully understood.

Over two millennia ago, according to legend, one such child was born in the tiny desert village of Qirmizia, which stood in the outer reaches of the fabled Kingdom of Scorching Sands. A baby boy by all appearances, the parents named the infant Saad and raised the newborn as a son. Yet it did not take them long to realize their child was entirely unlike all the little boys in their tiny village.

"You were correct in your suspicions," the village Healer told the parents, right before the child turned two. "I sense the soul of a daughter locked inside the body of a son."

"But how is that possible?" asked the father. "What could we have possibly done wrong?"

Historians recount that the Healer then laughed at the father's questions and said, "Sometimes blue-shelled oysters have pink flesh. Sometimes bulls prefer horns over hinds. And sometimes a lamb is born both ram and ewe. I doubt any of *their* parents made mistakes. These things are all just part of the natural order of our world."

Only a single sleepless night thereafter did the parents need to fully comprehend what they had learned, for their faith in the benevolent will of the Heavens above was absolute. And just after dawn the next morning, they woke their beautiful daughter and explained to her that from that day on, she would be called Sahar instead.

Life was good for Sahar for years thereafter. She was allowed to dress like all the other girls in the village, and she spent countless hours watching her mother practice the traditional dance of their people.

"One day, I'll get to teach you how to wind dance too," her mother told her.

"Why can't you just teach me now?" Sahar implored.

Smiling fondly down at her, Sahar's mother said, "You cannot take your rightful place among the Alriyahi until your Trials are complete. That is the way it has always been."

So for years, Sahar waited patiently for the exciting day when her parents would take her far across the desert to the sacred forest in the sands where, for untold centuries, the Trials of all her ancestors had taken place.

But it was in the midst of her twelfth winter when troubling news first came to the village. In the great city of Jauhara, to the east, Crown Prince Auren was to be summoned back from his Trials early following the death of his father, King Sinan the Cruel. But with no one to lead the Kingdom of Scorching Sands in the boy king's absence, every village along the vast border regions, including Sahar's own, would be vulnerable to raids from any number of unfriendly neighboring tribes.

The first attack on Qirmizia came sweeping in from the Askari Mountains in the middle of the night. With an obsidian moon looming ominously overhead, the raiders only sought to test the village defenses.

And three nights later, they attacked again—this time taking dozens of men, women, Anderen, and even children as their prisoners.

Yet it was on the ninth day, after incessant pleas from the people of Qirmizia to the capital for aid, when the Askari raiders unleashed their full fury on the village. Forced to defend themselves with minimal armaments, the people of Qirmizia together took up swords and shields, bows and arrows, all in a final, desperate attempt to protect their children and homes. Alas, even their most heroic efforts quickly turned out to be in vain.

Goldenfire flames and Ildarglass arrows rained down upon Qirmizia for hours on end that night, leaving Sahar cowering in fear with a large group of other children. Their screams of panic pierced the night when an Askari raider entered Sahar's home, an Ildarglass sword in hand. He never saw Sahar's mother coming. Brandishing an Ildarglass blade of her own, she appeared from thin air and shattered the intruder's soul with a single precise strike to his burning heart. An invisible shock wave of raw spectral energy exploded out within seconds, knocking Sahar and all the other children to the ground.

"Come with me," Sahar's mother commanded before grabbing three heavy satchels, each one overflowing with supplies. "We need to leave. Now!"

Using the last of her strength to keep the children concealed as they fled into the desert, she had nothing but the midnight sky above to guide her toward the nearest Ildarwood forest. For four long days they traveled, beneath the mild winter sun for hours on end, then amidst the bitter cold at night.

But when they arrived at last atop a mountainous dune in the middle of the desert, one major obstacle still remained.

"Why are there three forests?" asked Sahar, confused by what she saw on the horizon ahead.

"The Ildarwood in this desert is the only one for hundreds of miles around," her mother explained, "which means it must be protected to keep every child within safe. The only way to do that out here is to maintain a powerful illusion that only those with souls still Ildarbound will be able to see through. Were you actually old enough to start your Trials, you would be taken to the Ildarwood by one of the guardians in those woods—noble people we call Preceptors. But without their aid, I'm afraid you must try to reach the Ildarwood on your own."

"What do you mean, on our own?" Sahar asked with surprise.

"You will never be able to find the Ildarwood with me at your side. If that were possible, anyone could simply use a child to navigate this part of the Scorching Sands."

"But ... where will you go?" asked Sahar.

"Don't you worry about me," her mother insisted. "I will find my way to safety, one way or another. But you will need the rest of our supplies to reach those woods, so make sure to take good care of them, and try not to eat or drink everything that's left right away. You'll need to walk for another two days at least, assuming you don't get lost, which means you'll need to make every last drop and crumb count."

Heartbroken to have to leave her mother, Sahar said her final good-byes, then reluctantly continued with the other children from her village—their course set by the distant forests during the day and by the stars themselves at night.

The first day had passed before Sahar realized that her time to reach the Ildarwood was quickly running out. Seemingly no closer to the distant forests than she had been when her mother had remained behind, Sahar stood atop the nearest dune at twilight and hoped that the vanishing sun might help her narrow down which of the three forests was secretly true.

Yet only as she turned her attention back in the opposite direction did she notice a peculiar sight, for it appeared that the stars themselves were moving toward her. Thinking it either an illusion of the evening air or a hallucination from exhaustion, Sahar stared at the unusual movement until it finally took the shape of a young and handsome traveler.

"You are a long way from any shelter," the young man said once he arrived, a long white staff made of pristine Asterwood gripped firmly in one hand.

Only up close did Sahar finally recognize the man's elaborate shawl. A sacred garment worn by the Yadoshi peoples, it was made of a rare iridescent fabric that would turn jet black at night yet appear bright white in the warm light of day. But most stunning of all were the hundreds of tiny Ildarglass crystals woven carefully into the shawl to make it twinkle in the darkness like a midnight sky, while in the blazing heat of the midday sun, it would look like sparkling sand instead.

"Can you help us reach the Ildarwood?" Sahar asked the stranger. "Our village was attacked by Askari raiders, and my mother told us we would only find safety within the ancient woods."

"You are in luck," the Yadoshi man said with a smile. "My name is Adiv, and I happen to be an oath-sworn Preceptor of the Ildarwood."

He needed only a moment to retrieve a small mechanical device from his belt. On its metallic surface, tiny Ildarglass gems had been embedded in the shape of a unique compass rose—the sacred symbol of the Yadoshi people for untold centuries. And hovering just above the star was a glowing white needle made of a shimmering Ildarglass shard. "This will help us find the forest during the day, and it will guide us using the light of the stars at night."

Leading Sahar and the other children ahead, Adiv took great pleasure in answering all their burning questions—though none impressed him quite so much as the ones that came from young Sahar.

"So, your people believe the Sanctum Star will one day fall from the Heavens, but you don't know when or where it'll actually happen?" she asked at one point in the night, ever eager to learn.

"Some people of faith believe it has already fallen," said Adiv. "Others, like me, believe it will only appear when its Heavenly power is required for us to win the prophesied War for Ildaris, the World Beyond Our World. But until that day comes, we dedicate our lives to exploring *this* world in search of any peaceful souls who require either help or hope or justice. And only once we've helped enough people in need are we permitted to return to our ancestral home. Such is the Yadoshi way."

"My mother used to tell me stories about the Sanctum Star and all the other Sacred Relics," Sahar recalled fondly. "She said that a thousand years after the death of the First Mother, An'tumbe, and her children, their birthstones were taken from their graves and used to create the nine most powerful treasures ever made. She also said they've all been scattered around the world and lost to time."

"Your mother was right," said Adiv. "In the Golden City of Al-Dahabi, an ancient order called the Maktabat helps maintain the largest collection of scrolls and written knowledge the world has ever known. And there are supposedly entire sections dedicated to the Ancestral First and the Nine Sacred Relics. But I don't suppose you can actually recall what the other eight relics were."

Sahar grinned widely at the challenge. "The Relic of Light was called the Sanctum Star, and the Relic of Darkness was called the Blackheart Drum. The Relic of Fire was the Everburning Torch, and the Relic of Ice was called the Blizzard Horn. The Relic of Water was called the Tidal Trident, and the Relic of Storms was the Stormbound Spear. The Relic of Rock was the Unbreakable Hammer, and the Relic of Wind was called the Zephyr Chime."

"What about the Mother's Relic?" asked Adiv.

"That one was called the Sylvan Bell," Sahar answered proudly. "My mom said it was so powerful it could stop any battle or war with a single chime, but that it could only ever be rung once every thousand years."

"It sounds to me like mother and daughter both are very knowledgeable," Adiv said with a smile, earning a shy smirk from Sahar in turn.

"Do the Yadoshi know where any of the other eight relics are?"

"We have our suspicions," Adiv answered. "Nearly a thousand years ago, in the midst of a great war, it is said that the Stormbound Spear was stolen by Denycian soldiers and used to create a god so powerful that his armies were almost impossible to stop. Fearing what would happen if he ever got ahold of even one of the other relics, tribal leaders from all across Ondala agreed to send most of the rest to distant corners of the world. That way, no one people or faith could ever amass too much power over others.

"They say the Ondalans needed only the combined powers of the Sylvan Bell and the Blackheart Drum to defeat the invading forces, but even then, the Denycian armies and gods were so incredibly strong that the war was almost lost. After that, those last two relics remained in Ondala for centuries, until the bell was smuggled away to keep it safe."

"Have you ever seen one of the relics yourself?" Sahar asked eagerly.

"There's only one relic I want to see before I die, if only to gaze upon its beauty for an instant. But of course, if the legends are true, then for anyone to behold the Sanctum Star, it would mean that it had fallen from the Heavens, signaling the start of an age of endless war. So I suppose that also means I don't want *anyone* to ever see the Sanctum Star again."

Sahar stared up into the Heavens as she continued her lessons with Adiv until dawn. Only then did the three distant forests emerge on the horizon once more, bringing a timely end to a long night's travel.

Stopping briefly to make camp, Adiv and Sahar made sure everyone had the chance to eat and rest before they attempted to continue onward. But much to their shared dismay, the weary travelers barely had time to finish their meal before Adiv spotted something suspicious in the distance.

"Someone's coming," he warned the children. "And I suspect it might be raiders."

"How many?" Sahar asked nervously.

"Too many," Adiv replied.

So, with utmost haste, the travelers packed their belongings before swiftly hiding themselves at the base of the nearest dune.

Terrifying minutes passed as they each held their breath. It did not take long for the raiders to surround them all entirely.

With Ildarglass arrows drawn and ready, the raiders arrived on the backs of the most frightening Ildarian camels that Sahar had ever seen. Constructed from Ildarwood branches that were covered with cactus-like thorns, the creatures had burning amber crystals for eyes and long, sharp fangs like those of a saber-toothed cat.

"Please, fair travelers," said Adiv, "I am merely a humble Preceptor attempting to guide these lost sheep back to their flock within those most ancient and sacred of woods. We only wish to travel in peace."

Yet the raider captain was not so easily swayed. Instead, he leaped down from his mighty camel, drew his Ildarglass sword, and pressed its blade against Adiv's exposed neck.

"We have our orders. Everyone we find has to come back with us. There shall be no exceptions."

"I can offer you payment when we arrive," Adiv countered. "If you'll only escort us the rest of the way, I can assure you, it will be well worth your while."

The raider captain considered the request for only a moment. Then he pressed his blade so firmly against Adiv's neck that it began to bleed pure Silverblood. "You must think I'm a fool, far zindiq," the captain replied, using a crude Askari slur. "You could never find the woods in our presence, so you must intend to lead us into a trap!" An instant later, the captain shoved Adiv to the ground and readied his blade for one final, decisive strike.

"Leave him alone!" Sahar cried, launching herself in between the captain and her friend. "Please! We'll do anything. Just let us continue to the Ildarwood in peace."

The captain snorted and grabbed Sahar by the arm. "What have we here? A little boy trying to pretend he's a little girl? How pathetic!"

"I'm not a little boy," Sahar insisted, but the captain had heard enough.

"Take the rest. This muhtal needs to be put in his proper place."

The order had barely been given before Adiv blasted the captain with a powerful beam of spectral light, sending him up into the air and over the nearest dune. Then Adiv used his Asterwood staff to blind the remaining raiders before disarming them all, one by one.

"Hurry up and come with me," he told the children, taking one of the Ildarian camels by its reins and placing one hand against its thrashing head. "Lead us into the sacred woods, and I shall set you free," he told the creature, causing it to reluctantly calm and kneel. And within seconds, two other camels followed suit, choosing freedom over further enslavement by the brutal Askari hordes.

"Onto the camels, quick!" Adiv ordered.

"What about them?" asked Sahar, her gaze focused solely on the disoriented raiders. "Won't they die out here without camels or supplies?"

Adiv shook his head while staring back at her. "If they renounce their ways and turn to the Heavens for mercy, then an agent of the light will present themselves in time. But if they refuse to repent, then Heavenly justice will have been rightly served."

Sahar remained silent for hours after that, some small part of her relieved by the raiders' fate in light of their savage ways. Yet even though they were no longer a threat, she could not shake the lingering sting that their cruel words had irreparably left upon her soul.

"You're still upset about what the raider captain said, aren't you?" Adiv asked as the midday sun reached its peak.

Sahar immediately looked away. "My mom used to make sure I always looked like a girl when she was still around, but I guess I just forgot I still look like a boy without her help."

"This may come as some surprise, but you will not be the first cross-spirited child the sacred woods have ever seen," Adiv said warmly. "The forest will do its part to make sure others only ever see you the way you truly see yourself, but it never hurts to have a little extra help from some of the Preceptors you're bound to meet. They'll teach you how to perfect the illusion over time, until it's as real as real can be."

Sahar breathed a sigh of relief. As far as she was concerned, her long-awaited arrival in the Ildarwood could not possibly come soon enough.

Night descended upon the group again in the hours that followed, giving Adiv the final bearings he needed to guide the weary children through the remnants of the desert mirage at last. And staying true to his word once they finally entered the ancient forest, Adiv helped Sahar find a mentor who could fully restore her proper face.

"Your mother must've been Alriyahi," said the woman. "If you want to be just like her, we can teach you to master the art of casting illusions."

There was almost nothing that Sahar wanted more—except, of course, to see her beloved mother and father once again.

In the years that followed, Sahar dedicated her time in the Ildarwood to learning as much as she possibly could, beginning with a prompt mastery of her control over Crimsonwind. Only once she had finally learned to perfect her own appearance without the aid of special foods or artifacts did she turn her attention to learning more about the unique peoples and complex histories of the surrounding kingdoms.

It was in the midst of those studies that heartbreaking news arrived at her door. A full-scale war had broken out between the Kingdom of Scorching Sands and the militant tribes of the Askari Mountains. But most distressing of all were the smuggled-out memories of people from her home village, which was quickly becoming a fortified city in the enemy's growing empire. Such things were all the motivation she needed to redouble her search for any viable means to save her people.

Eight long years did Sahar end up spending in the Ildarwood, even though her Trials could have ended after four. Convinced that the deepest and most dangerous parts of the forest might finally contain the answers she had long sought, she reached the outermost edge of the

Ildarwood's perilous Direwood core before finally conceding defeat. Her desperate search for answers would need to continue somewhere else.

With her connection to the Ildarwood finally broken once her Trials were complete, Sahar joined Adiv on a pilgrimage across the Three Great Deserts until they arrived at last in the Golden City of Al-Dahabi. And on a fortified island within its harbor, they found the fabled Tower of Infinite Knowledge—the greatest lighthouse and collection of scrolls the world had ever known. With an enormous white Ildarstar shining brightly within its peak, the tower stood as an eternal monument to those who dared pursue brilliance, even in the darkest of times.

For weeks on end, Sahar consulted as many scrolls and maps as Adiv could find on the Nine Sacred Relics, the wars of various desert civilizations, and the complex history of the Askari Mountain tribes. But when none of those efforts proved fruitful, Sahar was forced to attempt something far more drastic—drinking a potentially lethal tea from the ancient library's Forbidden Well.

Despite being warned by Adiv that countless scholars had gone mad after drinking the fabled tea, Sahar proceeded down into the deepest catacombs beneath the tower until she arrived within a boundless cavern. Awestruck by the unimaginable sight before her, she stared with wonder at the true source of the tower's infinite knowledge—an enormous Sagewood tree, which was growing upside down from the chamber's crystal-covered ceiling. Drinking in an endless cascade of memories from every soul ever buried in the catacombs above, the tree combined countless lifetimes of knowledge with every last detail of information recorded in all the scrolls and maps on the library shelves. And some among the resident scholars in the tower had even begun to believe that the remarkable silver tree could also read the memories of any living soul who dared set foot on the island itself.

Guided by the oldest and wisest of the scholars, Sahar approached the tip of the tree as it lingered mere feet above the chamber floor.

"Once you touch the nearest leaf, you may either ask a question or state a problem. Do not let go until the leaf glows bright. Then merely pluck it from the branch and bring it to this altar. You must brew the tea alone and drink every last drop to receive whatever answer you so desperately seek."

Brave even in her uncertainty, Sahar approached the tree and reluctantly followed the scholar's instructions.

"I need to end the war between the Kingdom of Scorching Sands and the Askari. That way, no more innocent lives will be ruined. I just wish I knew how."

Sahar plucked the Ildarglass leaf once it finally achieved peak brightness. Then she cautiously proceeded to the ancient altar. Warned one last time about the tea, Sahar watched with awe as the shimmering silver liquid began to brew. And just as soon as it was done, she consumed it all in a single, decisive gulp.

Jarring memories from dozens of lost souls began to flash before Sahar's eyes, nearly driving her to madness over the course of seven days. It was not until the morning of the eighth that Sahar at last began to recover.

"I think I understand," she told Adiv before beginning the next leg of her fateful journey—this time, on her own.

From the Tower of Infinite Knowledge, Sahar traveled through the deep and perilous jungles of Ondala. There she met dozens of fascinating tribes, from those who lived off the land in small villages to those who lived in great walled cities of remarkable beauty.

High in the Ikamba Mountains, she met the Riyooyin—one of the oldest of Ondala's ancient Wind Tribes—who spent their days and nights burning the crimson buds of Windrose trees to surround themselves with mesmerizing illusions at all times. She swiftly discovered that they had little interest in any matters involving the physical world.

Next, Sahar continued down into the Damba River Valley, where she met another ancient Wind Tribe, the Shucuur. A nomadic people, they, too, spent their days in the company of incredible illusions, but unlike the Riyooyin, the Shucuur people preferred instead to use their gifts to tell stories. It was they who helped Sahar make her way at last to the vast Jojani Plateau.

Upon those great plains, Sahar found but a single mountain peak— the capital city of the Dabaya people. Here she found scholars and artisans of almost every variety, with schools and shops, enormous gardens, foundries, and more. And when she arrived within the central palace, she was greeted as an honored outsider by the royal family, who lived within.

Direct descendants of O'mehsi, daughter of An'tumbe herself, the king and queen treated Sahar to a lavish feast. But when the time came for Sahar to formally make her request for the whereabouts of the mythic Zephyr Chime, they both refused to give her the answer she so desperately sought.

Only after their first refusal did Sahar finally realize the error of her ways, for every member of the ancient Wind Tribes of Ondala she had met throughout her travels had been a storyteller in some way—from their illusions and tall tales to all their beautiful wares and crafts. So Sahar did what O'mehsi herself would have done, and in the center of the royal court, she began to dance. Performing the very same intricate movements her mother had demonstrated countless times before, Sahar used her gifts to create an illusion so incredibly realistic that all those present began to see firsthand the tragedy of Sahar's life, as well as what was happening to her people in the war.

Moved to tears by the story, Crown Prince Miraj was the one who rose in support of Sahar and her quest. "Tell me what you propose, and if I believe your plan will work, then I will take you to where the Zephyr Chime sleeps."

Some say Sahar needed only one night to convince the crown prince, while others say she required eight. Either way, her efforts to sway Prince Miraj to join her cause were a success, and once he finally agreed to accompany her, he tasked one hundred of his guards to prepare for the perilous trip ahead.

They would need three months to reach the portion of the vast Qahil Desert where the ancient relic was kept. After traveling back through the jungles of Ondala, they continued into the largest stretch of sand in the entire world. Battered by merciless windstorms whenever the scorching sun was not cooking them alive, Sahar and her escorts pressed on—despite seemingly endless exhaustion—until they reached the sacred site at last.

A towering obelisk made of ruby Ildarglass stood in the middle of nowhere, concealed to all except those wearing the protective crest of the Dabayan royal family. And in the very center of the obelisk hung the sparkling Crimsonwind chime.

Three more months did it take for Sahar and Prince Miraj to return to the outer reaches of the Askari Empire's ever-expanding borders. But with the ancient chime at their disposal, they were able to proceed safely across the Scorching Sands until they finally reached the fortified city of Qirmizia.

Gone was the tiny, defenseless village that Sahar remembered from her youth, for in its place stood a military stronghold of breathtaking size and grandeur. Constructed by thousands of captured Ildarstone masons from the Jabali Mountains, the city had become the crown jewel of the Askari Empire's desert frontier.

Yet as Sahar walked unseen through the bustling streets, she quickly realized that life for the enslaved populace was every bit as harsh and jarring as the Askari architecture all around them. And almost everywhere Sahar looked, she saw remnant souls from her childhood—nearly all of them either Broken or living in squalor.

Enraged by such sights, Sahar used the immense power of the Zephyr Chime to create an illusion unlike any other—though only for those who harbored true hatred in their heart for all the subjugated people within the city. Through the eyes of the oppressors, what descended upon Qirmizia was a horde as monstrous as Sahar could possibly imagine. Great winged beasts with terrifying fangs and razor-sharp claws soared through the skies and attacked without mercy, each one immune to the Askari soldiers' flaming weapons.

Fleeing the city by the thousands, the Askari ran out into the Scorching Sands with barely any camels or supplies. And as soon as the very last soldiers were outside the massive city walls, Sahar used the Zephyr Chime to create a powerful mirage of protection around the city, just like the one she had seen around the Ildarwood so many years before.

From that point onward, only those with Sahar's blessing would ever be able to find Qirmizia.

In the weeks that followed, Sahar arrived within the court of King Auren as the hero who had brought a swift and merciful end to the years-long war. Yet only once Sahar was absolutely certain that Auren was a far kinder king than his father did she pledge to him the loyalty of her city.

The ensuing decades would see a lasting peace as Qirmizia was joined by other neighboring settlements to create the fabled Hidden Cities, each one forever concealed by the seemingly inexhaustible power of the Zephyr Chime. And with Sahar the Wise as their leader, they grew into thriving centers of commerce and trade, where refugees from distant wars were always welcome.

According to ancient historians, Sahar was reunited with her parents not long after the end of the war. And in the years that followed, she was blessed with countless suitors, many of whom arrived with entire caravans full of treasure to try to earn the favor of the legendary Lady of the Veils. Yet our histories do not say with any certainty who finally claimed her ruby heart.

All we know is that she spent the remainder of her days beloved by all. And when she died at the remarkable age of one hundred and one, some say it was with a grieving partner at her side, while others claim it was instead a room overflowing with gorgeous, inconsolable lovers. But no matter which one was ultimately true, every trustworthy source has confirmed that Sahar died as she lived—smiling, cherished, and proud.

The Legend of Silvis

ACROSS THE MANY lands of our world, there are myths and legends that never leave their native borders. But every now and again, one will transcend cultures and take on a life all its own. Such is the case with the story of Old Silvis Synder.

Though few records from the Third Dark Age have survived, and Ildarwood trees from the time are fewer still, those that remain tell of a baby born near the heart of the Reichlands, somewhere just outside the vast and fabled forest of Freimuth. A place where magical things were said to happen, despite its great distance from the nearest Ildarwood, Freimuth Forest began to develop a far more sinister reputation in the year 8550, which many historians claim to be the definitive start of the Third Dark Age.

With plague and famine spreading rapidly across the continent of Iyteria, from each of the Old Kingdoms in the east all the way to the frigid tundra of Zimaria in the west, families in the area of Freimuth had begun to adopt a strange and tragic tradition. No one knows precisely how or when the practice first started, but it was around that fateful year in the eighty-sixth century when local constables began to notice starving children wandering about the forest.

Abandoned by their parents when food was so grievously scarce that extra mouths had become an existential threat, the children were taken deep into Freimuth Forest with what few supplies the family could spare in the hope that they might somehow learn to survive all on their own, just as they might in the Ildarwood. Alas, far too many children at the time failed to adapt to life in the savage wilderness.

But one who managed to succeed was a young Silvis Synder.

Only nine years old at the time, Silvis was born Anderen—a Reich-lander term derived from the name of the isle of Anderis, where legends spoke of a thriving populace of people who lived outside the traditional boundaries of "man" and "woman." With a soul that defied definition at birth, Silvis had always been an independent child. Far more interested in books than chores, Silvis had preferred the company of animals over people and purportedly claimed that the former were often far more civil. But when a severe lack of food forced their parents to make a heartbreaking choice, Mr. and Mrs. Synder decided to send young Silvis away with little more than a handful of books.

It is said that Silvis survived their first few years in Freimuth Forest scavenging and storing any mushrooms, berries, and nuts they could possibly find. And though less reputable sources have claimed that Silvis ate bugs and every manner of helpless woodland animal while living in a cave, no proof for such odious rumors has ever been found. Quite to the contrary, Silvis fatefully found their way to an abandoned cottage beside the raging Riegel River only three days after they were first abandoned in those woods.

Silvis had heard many stories about the infamous river while grow-ing up, though not a single one ever involved an outcome one might consider happy or good. As the only river in the region that flowed down in the direction of the nearest Ildarwood, it had become the site of countless sorrows during the worst years of the famine. With few other options at their disposal, families up and down the river had begun to leave their starving newborns and toddlers in floating baskets, each time praying to the Heavens above that their guiding hands would take the precious child into the protective arms of the Ildarwood miles downstream.

Few ever survived the trip.

So for years, Silvis was forced to watch as bundle after bundle slowly made its way down the river—some of them empty, and some still full—each time knowing it was impossible to save the precious life inside.

Silvis thought often about the Ildarwood and all the magical stories they had ever read about the fabled forest. Yet so petrified was Silvis of the countless dangers lurking within that, when the first day of spring after their twelfth birthday finally came, they never made the long and arduous trek downriver to officially begin their Trials. And as a direct result of that decision, they never learned how to control a spectral element, nor did their eyes ever change color from a simple silver-gray. And for most of their early life, Silvis never learned how to grow an Ildarwood tree or even how to ignite their first Ildarstar, leaving them especially vulnerable to every manner of threat.

For twenty long years, Silvis lived entirely alone. Their only interactions with people from the outside world occurred when the occasional hunter or lost traveler would wander too deep into the forest, forcing Silvis to hide out of fear. Yet every now and again, Silvis would wander into the nearest town under cover of darkness in desperate search of needed supplies. In this way, Silvis inadvertently created another legend—that of the Thieving Ghoul of Freimuth, although that is a story for another time. But it should still be noted that Silvis always made sure to leave what little food or tokens of perceived value they had to spare in exchange for whatever they had swiped.

The Third Dark Age seemed to come to a timely end in the twenty years since Silvis had arrived in Freimuth Forest, and with fewer and fewer children being abandoned to the vast woodlands—and almost no infants being sent downstream—Silvis could only conclude that food had finally become less scarce. And by the time Silvis neared their thirtieth birthday, they had even begun to hope that a time might soon come when no children at all were abandoned within the vast borders of Freimuth or along the Riegel River.

But alas, Silvis quickly discovered that all their hopes were entirely in vain.

Hundreds of miles away, in the castles and keeps of a dozen high lords and would-be kings, an ancient corruption had begun to fester. Fed by lingering suffering and remnant scars from the early years of the Third Dark Age, the corruption twisted the minds of those already prone to fear, whilst igniting fresh fires in the hearts of all who bathed their souls in hate and violent fury.

Rumors began to spread of a vast and insidious Blight infecting large swaths of the nearest Ildarwood, as well as all the other Ildarwoods in countries far beyond. And so the people of the Reichlands began to panic, for none among them wanted the Third Dark Age to resume. But what could they possibly do to prevent such calamitous fortunes?

The corrupted high lords and would-be kings all had an answer— one purportedly whispered to them in the night by the twice-fallen gods of darkness and war. And from their great castles, the ruthless rulers each loudly proclaimed that every terrible thing happening across the once-thriving Reichlands was irrefutably the fault of all the peculiar people they called "the Others."

"Those strange, insidious creatures who are nothing like the rest of us," said some.

"Aberrations in the eyes of the Heavens," said many more.

But most damning of all were the slanderous claims that drove otherwise reasonable men and women into fits of needless panic and uncontrollable rage. The lie often whispered in taverns before being shouted in large crowds by demagogues, tyrants, and fiends: "They're coming for your children!"

A wave of terror swept through every corner of the Reichlands thereafter, beginning with mass roundups of every "unusual" soul that people could find. The first ones gathered were immediately left Broken, their souls ruthlessly shattered—often by Ildarglass swords or spectral flames, though sometimes only after days or weeks of suffering. Then came the killings—something rarely ever seen in the history of our world.

For over eight millennia, ever since the Dawn of the Ancestral First, the consequences of killing any innocent person or beast without just cause were catastrophically clear. Such a death would immediately spread corruption into the souls of those nearby, leading only to more death and an inevitable Blight. So from the earliest days of civilization, whether in wars or matters of justice, cultures in almost every land chose instead to punish solely by shattering souls.

Of course, Silvis had no knowledge of what was happening outside Freimuth Forest or why. All they knew was that babies and toddlers had once again begun flowing down the river, day after day, while older children still too young for their Trials were being abandoned with alarming regularity inside the woods.

One such child was a quirky little girl named Rayna.

First discovered while Silvis was foraging for food just before the start of winter, Rayna was only eleven years old and utterly terrified when Silvis first appeared. Dressed in the ratty old clothes of a boy, she had short black hair and sparkling violet eyes, leaving Silvis visibly startled at first sight of her too. So it should come as no surprise that both promptly fled in panic.

Seeking refuge in their patchwork cottage, Silvis resolved to stay put for at least a day or two, lest they have another surprise encounter with the unusual little girl. Much to the surprise of Silvis, however, Rayna had followed them back to the cottage, and as soon as she was entirely certain that Silvis was no true threat, she decided to knock upon their door.

"Go away!" Silvis commanded. But Rayna chose not to listen.

"You dropped a lot of berries when you ran away," Rayna ever so gently replied. "I just wanted to bring them back so you don't run out of food."

Silvis was at a loss for words. Slowly opening the old wooden door, they stared down at the girl and could hardly believe their eyes. Not once since being sent into the forest had anyone shown Silvis a single act of kindness. Not until that very day.

"What happened?" Silvis asked from a seat beside their greenwood fire, though only once Rayna was at last invited in. "How did you end up here?"

"My mom and dad brought me," Rayna somberly replied. "They said people are mad. They think kids like me will be dangerous when we grow up, so they're trying to find as many of us as they can. That way, they can Break us, or worse."

"People like you?" asked Silvis. "You mean little girls?"

"No. I mean people who don't look or act like everyone else. They're calling all of us the Others. The Anderen. And it sounds like they want every last one of us dead."

The Anderen. It was a phrase that Silvis had not heard for over twenty years. "So you were abandoned, just like me?" Silvis said with a heavy heart.

"My mom said she was saving my life," Rayna answered. "She said some parents were turning their Anderen kids over, and others were just kicking them out. But she didn't want anything bad to happen to me, so she gave me a bag full of food and brought me out here. Then she told me to just follow the river downstream till I finally reached the Ildarwood."

Silvis could hardly believe their ears. "I don't have much to give you, but you can take some food and dry wood to help you on your way."

"You mean, I can't stay here with you?" Rayna asked desperately, deathly afraid of having to continue for miles on her own.

Silvis stood silent in disbelief. "I ... have almost nothing. And people … I have books … lots of books … but people—I don't like people …"

"Wait … how long have you been out here all by yourself?"

Silvis froze for several moments before pointing to a row of narrow lines that had been carved into the wall. "This will be my twenty-first winter."

Rayna gasped, her heart nearly broken by the confession. But then she reached into her satchel and retrieved two small tomes she had brought with her. "I have a couple good books, and I can help you find more food. My father taught me to hunt and how to fix our house, so maybe we could actually help each other out."

Silvis stared at the young girl, speechless. And though the very thought of having to care for a child left Silvis terrified, they finally agreed to let Rayna stay.

The winter that followed was unusually harsh, but Silvis was amazed to discover how much easier to endure the heavy snows were with just a little extra help. And once most of the worst holes in the cottage roof and walls were patched—though barely so—Silvis and Rayna kept each other company and used their endless hours together to help each other learn.

But when the coming spring had nearly arrived at last, Silvis decided it was best to help Rayna continue on her journey. After taking her all the way to the edge of the nearest Ildarwood forest, miles and miles downstream from the patchwork cottage, Silvis said a tearful goodbye and wished her luck. And though Silvis would immensely miss her company, they wanted nothing more than to ensure Rayna would have the chance they never gave themself—to start and finish their Trials, and perhaps one day lead a normal life.

The solitude of Silvis would persist for only a few weeks before they found another stray child wandering helplessly through the woods—this one far younger than Rayna. And for days on end, Silvis refused to intervene, just as they had so many times before. But when the child unexpectedly found their way to the riverside cottage, Silvis again felt compelled to take them in.

Such was the life of Silvis for years on end. No sooner would they release one child out into the Ildarwood than another one, two, or even three would arrive and take their place. But with each new child that Silvis took in, the patchwork cottage grew, and Silvis gradually learned more about the outside world.

And by the time Rayna had finally returned to check on Silvis, just as soon as her Trials were through, half a dozen children were living with them—including a toddler who had just turned two.

"He washed up during a storm, and his basket was broken," Silvis explained when Rayna expressed her immense surprise. "I didn't know what else to do."

Rayna shook her head with astonishment over how much had changed before finally showing Silvis the two little gifts that she had brought. Forever grateful for what Silvis had done to save her all those years before, Rayna presented the smallest gift first. Resembling an opalescent pearl, it was the dormant seed of a Euwood tree—a rare type of Ildarwood with bark and leaves of every color. It had become a common symbol of hope as Anderens all over the Reichlands were hunted and oppressed by angry mobs.

"I think it's time," Rayna told Silvis before planting the tree together in the center of the house. It needed only a small amount of Silver from her soul to germinate and sprout before their eyes.

Next, Rayna presented the larger of the two gifts—an opalescent stone that barely fit in the palm of her hand. "This is the heart of a rare Ildarwood tree," she told Silvis. "Let me show you how to use it to ignite an Ildarstar."

"But ... won't that just make it easier for more kids to find me?" Silvis asked nervously.

"Would saving another life really be such a terrible thing?" Rayna promptly replied.

Finally convinced, Silvis accepted the crystal into their hands, then followed Rayna's instructions to make it ignite. And after a few nerve-wracking moments, they watched with wonder as the small silver sphere slowly took its place in the makeshift Asterport on the roof.

"Where will you go?" Silvis asked the next morning, just as soon as Rayna was preparing to leave. "It doesn't sound like the world outside these woods is very safe, so you're more than welcome to stay here."

"I really can't," Rayna replied. "Someone has to go out there and fight for our people."

"But they might *kill* you," Silvis whispered, hoping the nearest children would not hear.

"I know," Rayna said somberly. "But if I don't at least try, then who's going to stop the same terrible people from trying to kill *them* once their Trials are through?"

It was a thought more heartbreaking than Silvis could possibly bear.

"Please, just … visit if you can."

"At least once a year from now on. I promise," Rayna said with a smile.

Silvis never saw her again.

The years that followed took their toll on Silvis, with each fall bringing with it new visitors who had finished the Trials. But few promises to return were truly kept, and Silvis knew precisely the reason why. The violence outside the forest had only worsened with time.

"You might not be safe here for much longer," said Faron, one particularly kind returning child. "Our newest king has heard rumors of hidden houses all over the Reichlands. 'Places where the Others are still corrupting the hearts and minds of innocent children.' And now his words have started to infect the hearts of people in the Ildarwood too … including some of the children."

"But not *my* children," Silvis replied, their words desperately torn between a firm declaration and a question to which they did not ever want an answer.

"A few of them," said Faron, their head lowered in shame. "I'd like to think they'd never report you to anyone, but the fires of hatred are spreading quickly, even throughout those woods. Some people are even starting to call it the Golden Blight. And if it doesn't stop soon, I'm pretty sure it'll lead to war."

Silvis turned their attention toward a sleeping infant in its makeshift crib. It was impossible to believe such a sweet and innocent child could ever grow up to hate someone like Silvis after years of protection and selfless love.

"I can't just run away," said Silvis. "Where would I go?"

"What about the Ildarwood?" Faron suggested. "There are still parts that are considered safe, especially in the deeper woods."

"But ... then who would find all the lost children out here?"

Faron sighed with remorse. "Maybe it's finally time for you to just take care of yourself and stop worrying about everyone else."

Silvis considered Faron's words of advice for weeks thereafter before ultimately deciding not to heed them. But all the while, foul whispers at last began to spread through all the villages inside and around the fabled forest.

"Have you heard the rumors?" the whispers so routinely began. "There's an old witch who eats children somewhere out in those woods."

Others spoke of a monstrous creature with a limp and humped back that would wander into villages at night and steal infants. Some parents even began to blame "the Beast of Freimuth Forest" for taking the children they themselves had decided to banish, all in an effort to remove any lingering suspicions from those who might cast judgment. But the one thing those families all feared most was not the stigma of abandoning a child—it was the stain of having one of "the Others" born into their pure and precious bloodline.

And so, by winter's end, a deep and paralyzing fear had finally begun to creep into the patchwork cottage, leaving Silvis Synder convinced that the time would soon come when their home and all their innocent children would inevitably fall prey to a brutal attack.

Weeks of heavy snow had finally melted by the time dozens of villagers decided to enter the fabled forest. Carrying Ildarglass swords and a mix of torches alight with either pure or spectral flames, some even brought with them talismans of hope in the shape of an elaborate eight-point star. Fearing the dark and bewitching powers of the "creature in the woods," they were led by a man of the faith—a pale-skinned Astyrgard with bright white eyes and streaks of gray flowing here and there through his golden hair.

"We will use the sacred light of the Heavens and the cleansing fires of righteous fury to purge these woods!" he declared, rallying the villagers to follow him deep into the forest.

Silvis did not dare put up a fight.

Watching from afar as the patchwork cottage was burned to the ground while villagers celebrated and wept with joy, Silvis knew better than to ever risk shedding a tear. Instead, they simply guided all their remaining children down to the Ildarwood, then implored the oldest ones to help the youngest somehow find a home.

Returning to the depths of Freimuth Forest in defeat, Silvis took what few possessions of value they had managed to store away and brought them to a cavern so incredibly remote that no one—not even lost children—could ever find it.

And for several decades, that is precisely where Silvis remained. Out of danger. Out of sight. And out of mind.

Silvis was old and feeble by the time their secret cavern was discovered at last, once again by an unusual child in dire need. All the child wanted was somewhere warm and safe to sleep, plus any meager scraps of food that Silvis could spare. But alas, the tragic life of Silvis had left them miserable, and they had suffered far too much to risk any further heartbreak.

Nevertheless, the child persisted. And for an entire week straight, Silvis refused to offer any shelter.

It was on the ninth day when Silvis finally found them sleeping silently outside the cavern. Freezing and pale from the overnight cold, they had fallen deathly ill, forcing Silvis to decide the child's fate right then and there. Many sleepless nights followed as Silvis fought to save the child's life, and for weeks thereafter, Silvis begged for their forgiveness.

For three long years, Silvis took care of the kindhearted child, teaching them everything they needed to know to survive on their own. Then at last the time finally came for the child to start their Trials.

One last journey did Silvis make back to the Riegel River—their only one since the night their patchwork cottage had been burned down. Too heartbroken to bear the sight of the rubble, Silvis had avoided the spot for decades, ever fearful of what they might find.

Words could not express their surprise upon seeing what had transpired while they were gone. From the ashes of the cottage, an enormous Ildarwood tree had grown, ten times taller than the one Silvis had planted with Rayna all those years before. And around its base were countless offerings—beautiful flowers planted by children that Silvis had saved, as well as little stuffed animals and lots of faded notes of thanks. Remnants of candles long ago exhausted had left a thousand puddles of wax in a circle along the ground, and there in the center of it all was a stone plaque someone had left in memory of the person who had saved their life.

Moved to tears by the heartwarming display, Silvis fell to their knees and wept shamelessly. But because they had never learned to see the resulting Silver mist left floating in the air, they had no way of knowing that the shimmering streams had begun to spread out in all directions, each one flowing ever so gently toward every living soul who still thanked Silvis for taking them in.

Silvis completed one last journey to the Ildarwood that day. And after a tearful goodbye, they mustered the last of their strength to hobble all the way back to what had once been their patchwork home. Their final act was to lie down in the spot where they had spent so many lonely nights before, and they allowed themself to dream one final time.

And though the years and sacrifices had been particularly hard for Silvis, when they quietly passed in their sleep in the middle of the night, they did so knowing in their heart that, in the end, they had truly been loved.

THE GOLDEN BLIGHT left lingering scars upon the people of the Reichlands for generations thereafter, but the efforts of Silvis and countless "Others" played an integral role in saving thousands of lives.

By the time of Silvis's death, the word "Anderen" had evolved from a term of hatred towards *all* who were different, and it became one of reverence, particularly for those rare souls who defied the traditional bounds of "man" and "woman" and were quite simply unique. In due time, the word even began to be used by people all over the world, especially those who had grown up hearing incredible stories about all the heroic deeds of brave Anderens.

And though a few unfortunate folk tales still popped up in different cultures here and there—most about old witches or terrifying ghouls who enjoyed kidnapping stray children in a dark and magical forest—the true events of Silvis's life had a far more profound impact on the world at large.

When stories began to spread about the kindly Anderen who had taken in every unwanted child that had stumbled upon their door, people in disparate nations began to build special shelters in their honor. That is why, to this very day, so many homes for lost or orphaned children in every part of the world are overseen by at least one Anderen—someone who has dedicated their life to making sure such innocent souls are *always* safe and loved.

And in the center of those homes, there will nearly always be found a very special Ildarwood tree in memory of Silvis—one with bark and leaves of every color. An eternal symbol of hope and genuine appreciation for all of life's infinite diversity.

Timeline of Key Events

The following timeline includes all major events referenced in this book, plus some additional noteworthy events since the Dawn of the Ancestral First, working forward from the earliest confirmed event in recorded history.

Dawn of the Ancestral First, ~9,000–10,000 Years Ago: An'tumbe and her children are born. The children are banished into the jungles of Ondala at the age of twelve. After several years together, they go their separate ways and join other tribes across the Ondalan continent.

1 AS (Anno Spectris): The oldest written account of the Story of the Ancestral First is inscribed into a stone monument beside An'tumbe's burial tree.

~1500–4000 AS: The Age of Spectral Expansion. Descendants of the Ancestral First spread throughout the world. Their bloodlines become highly sought after.

~4000 AS: The Age of Religious Foundations begins. Faiths previously restricted to tribes and small regions around the world begin to expand.

~6000 AS: "The Legend of Arcus" takes place in the Nine Seas of Denycia.

~7000 AS: "The Legend of Sahar" takes place in the Kingdom of Scorching Sands.

~7100 AS: Lord Luciyen first appears to the people of Astyria, claiming to be a prophet from the Heavens. The first Astyrian Empire is founded.

~7950 AS: The Age of Global Conquest begins. Empires around the world attempt to expand. Refugees flee to Nacoryn countries in record numbers.

8550–8625 AS: "The Legend of Silvis" takes place in the Reichlands.

8740 AS: Astyrian forces invade the Selyrian Union and Alushaan Alliance.

8871 AS: The wars between the Astyrian Empire, the Selyrian Union, and the Alushaan Alliance come to an end. The Elyshan Ascendancy is formed from the remnants of the Alushaan Alliance.

8930 AS: The Great Elyshan War begins between the newly formed Elyshan Empyre and neighboring Nacoryn nations, including the Selyrian Union. Native Alushaan populations are nearly wiped out by non-native Elyshans.

8939 AS: The Great Elyshan War ends in a truce, but skirmishes continue for the next century.

8987 AS: The Great Blight spreads into Ranewood's portion of the Ildarwood from other parts of the forest.

8991 AS: The Last Maiden ends the Great Blight within Ranewood's borders.

8992 AS: The Last Maiden's home is burned down in Miner's Reach.

9039 AS: The Reign of Astyria ("the Reign of Stars") begins. The Astyrian Empire conquers most of the Selyrian Union and parts of the Elyshan Empyre.

9055 AS: The Massacre at Dead End in Ranewood takes place.

9058 AS: The Astyrian War ends when Astyrian forces withdraw from all captured territories in the Selyrian Union and the Elyshan Empyre.

9068 AS: *The Trials of Ildarwood: Fall of the Forsaken* (Chapters 1–9).

9087 AS: The Fall of Silvermarsh (*The Trials of Ildarwood: Fall of the Forsaken*, Epilogue; *The Trials of Ildarwood: Spectres of the Fall*, Prologue).

9088 AS: The Dulanes arrive in Amberdale.

9089–9090 AS: *The Trials of Ildarwood, Origins: Cinders in the Snow* (Chapters 1–7, Epilogue).

9091 AS: *The Trials of Ildarwood, Book One: Spectres of the Fall* (Chapters 1–26).

Made in the USA
Columbia, SC
21 November 2024

47140829R00136